FAST LANES

Jayne Anne Phillips

FAST LANES

E. P. DUTTON/SEYMOUR LAWRENCE
NEW YORK

Lyrics on page 64 from "Be My Baby" by Jeff Barry, Ellie Greenwich, and Phil Spector used by permission. Copyright © 1963 Trio Music Co., Mother Bertha Music Inc., and Warner-Tamerlane Publishing Co. All rights reserved.

Lyrics on page 110 from "Blue Moon" by Richard Rodgers and Lorenz Hart used by permission. Copyright 1934, renewed © 1962 Robbins Music Corporation. Rights assigned to CBS Catalogue Partnership. All rights controlled and administered by CBS Robbins Catalog Inc. All rights reserved. International copyright secured.

These stories have been previously published in *Esquire, Granta, Ploughshares, Rolling Stone, Gallimaufry, Best American Short Stories,* and *Pushcart Prize IV.* "How Mickey Made It" was first published as a limited edition by Bookslinger Editions. "Fast Lanes" was first published as a limited edition by Vehicle Editions.

Published in the United States by E. P. Dutton/Seymour Lawrence, a division of NAL Penguin Inc., 2 Park Avenue, New York, N.Y. 10016.

Library of Congress Cataloging-in-Publication Data   Phillips, Jayne Anne, 1952–   Fast lanes.   Contents: How Mickey made it—Rayme—Fast lanes—[etc.]   I. Title.   PS3566.H479F37   1987   813'.54
86-19959

ISBN: 0-525-24515-4

Published simultaneously in Canada by
Fitzhenry & Whiteside Limited, Toronto

W

DESIGNED BY EARL TIDWELL

10 9 8 7 6 5 4 3 2 1
First Edition

For Mark

The author wishes to thank
the National Endowment for the Arts
for support during the writing of this work.

CONTENTS

I have begun my freedom and it hurts.

—ALAN DUGAN
"Stability Before Departure,"
from *Collected Poems*

HOW MICKEY MADE IT

*T*his bed is wicked comfortable, I mean I sleep like a baby and don't wanna wake up. I guess you OWN a bed like this when you're twenty-eight huh (smile, tawny skin, fine sharp face) and this place is so CLEAN, nothin outa place but your head. Just kidding Darling, don't get hot (lighting his cigarette, frowning over cupped hands). No I mean older women are fine with me, you're fine with me really, a little awesome but I'll call you Mom once in a while just to keep us in line (inhaling, looking up with smoke on his lips). But don't pull any teen-ager numbers on me, that's all in the past,

remember I'm twenty now, that's, uh, TWEN-TEE—
you remember, a week ago when you gave me that
book of jokes, those cartoons? in the bar, handed it
right over the counter with the little sketch inside of
me in my nifty bartender's coat & cardboard bow tie
compliments of Savio's, what? yeah, she remembers,
signed it *with love from your customer* Happy Birthday
Mickey. Look just because we got a little boozed when
you took me to lunch that next day, and you said I
should call in sick so we could go to the beach, doesn't
mean you're RESPONSIBLE for me. I mean if they
fired me for that they were going to fire me anyway,
I shoulda given them a better excuse but what the fuck
it was a suckass job to begin with. I only had it the
month I've been back from England, just bread till I
get a band together. I've been fired plenty from everywhere without your help, so don't get pent up about
it. I'll get another job tomorrow, don't worry about
Mickey (shakes his head, black curls cut short on top
& long in the back, Galahad punk) I mean I haven't
been on my own since I was twelve for nothin, I can
get BY you know—I'm a kid but I try real hard.

Ooh, that is intense. That is so intense . . . softer, a
little softer, there. Oh, you feel good. . . . Relax, we're
OK, really, I'll pull out. . . . Take it easy, I'm nowhere
near coming—

Yeah for a while I was modeling downtown, what a
racket that shit is—guys smearing makeup all over
your face, three of them at once while you're sitting in
a chair (stands up out of bed, pulls on black denim
pants, white undershirt) and some other guy is brush-
ing your shoes then it's Stand up Pull in Turn Stop
Splat (flexing his long hard legs, goofing on a Marl-
boro smoker stance) HERE'S the smile you push GOT

IT KID?? you better get it. You see I had this whole whatsis portfolio expensive shit and I walked right in and got the job and the others were pissed, really quite the pisser when they'd been licking ass for weeks to get in the office. But after it was all over—four weeks I did it—I burned the whole thing, the job the pictures the assholes, all of it, and I told that fag to get himself another boy. I mean, can you see it, some chumpy fag drooling over those pictures. Suit, swimsuit, towel around the neck, what bullshit, I never played tennis in my life. I'm a SINGER I don't go for that commercial shit I'LL DO IT MYSELF THANK YOU, Thaaannk Yooooooo!!! Whoo! Jesus.

Doncha like to walk down the street with me, hmmm, doncha? Whoops, somethin tells me you're not amused, not amused HEY well excuse me (dodging passersby with elaborate swoops and fast two-step skips) I'm part preppie, can't help sliding through crowds, stay close now, we want everyone to know we're TOGETHER and we're RIGHT and we're COOL, Yoo Hoo, Everyone, This is MY FRIEND, This Girl (pointing, taking off in a sleuth's mince), Here, give HER the prize. Come, Darling. This way darling. And don't drag your feet, I can't AFFORD another pair of Candie's this week . . . keeping you in french ticklers keeps food from my mouth as it is. . . . Sweetheart, your kicks are killing me, why can't you be satisfied with that Malaysian dwarf I bought you? Ouch, OK, don't kick the shins, need the shins, STAGEWORK you know, you gotta Stand Up to project, I got the message, I'll shut up, we'll just walk. HEY EVERYONE, we're WALKING here, we're just WALKING. Wow, I love the street. See this lady in front of us with her kid crawling under its own stroller? Hey, she loves the day she loves that kid she

loves HER LIFE you can tell. Jesus, look at that face
—they ought to lock her up before she walks in front
of a truck—

OK here we are, take a good look, this is CHEAPO'S
—Only place to buy records in this town. Darling?
Sweetheart? Come back DARLING, Mickey's gonna
buy you some MU-SIC, he's gonna pay for his SUP-
PER, cut you off from that commercial dark ages
Stones shit (dancing in doorway, bowing from the
waist), Come IN now, don't be shy, never too late for
the good stuff, just don't get LOST now that we're on
the BRINK (running down aisles in smooth reggae
skip) OUH! (making faces, doing an imitation club-
foot) I hurt myself, I'm SUING. Now you see that cute
punky girl at the counter? She's going to spin some
tunes for us, hey, see? (lays out a dollar a record tip)
here are the imports, the real stuff, there's no real shit
over here, it's all happening in England like I told you.
Now listen I'm gonna get her to play The Members,
oh oh or hmmmm (sucking his finger, rolling his eyes)
ahhh, The Spectator—this cut with the fabulous Moog
that drifts off like balloons. You're gonna LIKE IT, it's
gonna Change Your Life, you'll be a rock 'n' roll baby
—You can't take it in at first, it sounds bitter maybe
but when you HEAR it you know what it is all at once
. . . and that doesn't mean you go out and buy yourself
a string tie and put on some *fashion* pose, just means
you KNOW what the real music is and you'll go where
you need to go to get it, like, look at these asshole
album covers, you can SEE what shit they're playing
by the sparkly lights on their jeans and how they hold
their fuckin streamline chromeline guitars like giant
cocks—it's sickening man and people buy this shit.
You see these imports. One little rack of singles with
penciled-in titles, but this shit is REAL this is REAL

music and they don't have to pretend it's sex. Yeah, balls, the family jewels.

I don't know I just never got along with my family, I mean they're not my family really since I'm adopted but they are my family—and it was always weird man, I mean they told me I was adopted from the start but still, all those years it was like, uh, how come *I* got such dark skin and how come I just don't really FEEL it for you. When I was fourteen they gave me the address of the adoption agency and I found out I'm half Comanche and half Spanish. I wrote four letters, four different letters man, and the agency sent me this long sheet of paper inscribed with the facts, but no names. I was born in Tucson, and my younger sister too, but she's no blood relation. Only the oldest one, my older sister, is their own kid, and Jesus it was always obvious. I mean, who graduated from Barnard, who works for ecology and married a lawyer? Not Mickey, man. Mickey got boarded off at the age of twelve because he was a mean little kid and always in fights. NO, I ain't gonna do it cause YOU say so man I mean who the fuck are YOU? And my younger sister, she's a case, she's fat, she sits all day in the easy chair and watches TV like a TV machine. Makes me sick—I tell her, I've told her, get off your butt, it's plain you hate yourself. Not me man. I love Mickey. Who cares if THEY love Mickey—that's why I said I've had it with this shit and I went to England when I was sixteen and lived with Nate. Nate, the kid I played basketball with at Wakefield High, after I came back from Correction School where I got CORRECTED Ha Ha. But Nate man, he was wonderful. England was really real, I *grew up* over there, I learned about rock 'n' roll. We went out to the pubs and the bars and we had a band and I got into singing. There I was, sixteen and really alive while everybody back here from my old street was asking daddy for the car, oh please daddy can I? ah come on Dad, I wanna get my hand in someone's pants in the backseat and have her home by 12:30 with her dress buttoned up right so *her* daddy don't ask questions. What? Yeah, I was singing, SINGING, S-I-N-G-I-N-G and living with a nice twenty-nine-year-old lady who had a little half-black kid that called ME daddy. Yeah, you see? Quite the difference.

I went to England to stay with Nate and he was living with Clytie, she was going to marry him so he could stay in the country, but I don't know, I just fell for her and Nate moved out with hard feelings but things settled and were cool in a few weeks—Clytie was so smart and hardheaded but crazy enough to put up with me, and had no real set on how anything should be—that's what *smart* is, you know? She shared this two-family flat with her dad and he drove a lorry and picked up scrap to sell. I mean it was two separate flats but her dad was around a lot and she did his meals and he gave her dough. She had grown up with her mother and found her father right after she'd had her baby, this beautiful brown kid she called Feather though his name was really Frederick. Her dad was just a working-class stiff but Clytie could do that, show up after twenty-five years with a half-black baby and make her father love her, and he was cool about her boyfriends. Boyfriends moved in and out and it's not true that kind of number always fucks kids up. Feather was happy, sunny cocoa face, about two and starting to talk. Nate and me took him to the club we worked, he watched while the group played. What a time that was. I'm sixteen and Escaped: school, family, house, and got what I want after *all that time* of bad-boy guilt trips. Nothin but YOU GOT NO FEELINGS FOR PEOPLE MICKEY, YR DAD AND I HAVE GIVEN YOU ALL

WE CAN BUT YOU DON'T KNOW WHAT TO DO
WITH IT DO YOU MICKEY and the day I got them
to release me on my own recognizance from the state
ward crap was the luckiest day of my life. I go to
England and there's Clytie, pale complexion and black
hair cut real short, so she looks like a boy almost,
except she's nursing and has these round, heavy
breasts. Nothing was dirty to Clytie, nothing was
stained or fucked up. She showed me about the feeling
of feeding a kid, that it pulled at her inside like a real
faint coming and made her wet. Evenings she would
be feeding Feather and I would lay down with them
and fall asleep from the suckling sounds. I was out at
night and she was out in the days sometimes, art-
modeling, and I took care of the baby. He did, he
called me daddy. Now, can you dig how that was for
me? I mean, I knew a lot, I'd been OUT THERE a long
time, but I didn't know this good stuff, always before
I only had glimpses, BAM, quick flash and close the
shutter—ah, there, THAT'S REAL—but only for a
minute, an hour maybe. I really pushed man, I pushed
to get in where the juice was.

The women I've cared about are mostly good women,
but I got no illusions about girls in general. You think
women don't use men for fucking? Bullshit, plenty of
women have used me for sex, just want some big cock
to bang their brains out, want you to walk around with
them all dressed up because you got a nice hard ass in
your pants, they got no feelings for you. Katrin, this
other girl I know—the one I met in the bar before I
met you, I told you about her—she's not like that,
she's a nice little girl, punky and kind and shy under
her red lipstick. She lives with her folks, that was her
dad's car I borrowed yesterday. Her family has plenty
and Katrin wants to pay for an apartment for me, I
mean she would still live at home but she would have

a place to go at times, you know? What d'ya mean? She knows me, I've been honest with her, she knows how I feel about the jealous maniac number, no, Katrin is cool. Besides, I've got about eighty bucks left and none of the clubs around here are going to let me bartend right off. You got to work up through the ranks just like in a fucking bank—barback and bus and whatever else they want to rankle you with. If I have to spend my dough on just living, rent and that shit, I'll never get enough money to split and do what I have to do. You think I'm wrong? How the fuck can you be me, how can you *do* that? You, with your life all peachy. Just let me be here, OK? let ME figure it out, I'm experienced.

My first real time was with a neighborhood girl the fall that I was twelve, I got into a lot of trouble over it. She had this big backyard with all these apple trees like a forest and we were back there in the trees, just innocent pushing against each other, feeling pretty loopy, like the first time you're tipsy on booze. She was leaning against a tree and had pulled me against her and her dress was up between us. She had unzipped my pants and then suddenly everything *fit,* you know, sounds like a joke, I mean I wasn't trying to fuck her, I didn't know I could fuck anybody, but she was one of these girls who all of a sudden catches fire and then doesn't know where she is. I mean there ARE such girls. Right then her mother has seen us from the house through the trees and starts SCREAMING the girl's name across the yard, yelling with this hysterical warble in her voice, and I was sort of pulling the girl around the tree so the mother couldn't see us when I slipped inside, really inside her, almost by accident. I will never forget it, I was amazed, she came, just in seconds, and I was watching her face the whole time. I didn't know what coming was and for a long time after that I thought there was something wrong with me because I hadn't felt the shaking SHE'D felt, with her eyes wide open but she wasn't there. Real scary, like the sky cracking open. By the time her mother got from the second floor of the house and across the yard to us it was all over—it was the mother who had worked up a passion and she kept on with it for several days. You might say the whole mess contributed to my parents' decision to get Mickey OUT, like once a dog has tasted blood he keeps on killing chickens. So they packed me off to where there were no chickens they'd know about—they gave up on me and made me a ward of the State. I was TWELVE man, with the whole puberty thing crashing around my head. I mean, CONFUSED? I was crazy, here was this totally heavy punishment when SHE was the one who had done that weird shaking. Had *I* done that to her, I mean I only just touched her in this softness and she exploded. And really the PACK HIM OFF gig was already in motion before that, I'd been in fights with some older boys and I'd done some petty stealing, but the actual change of residence came right on the heels of magic in the forest. Magic Mickey, what a laugh, it wasn't any magic I knew about till it grabbed me. Later I did the grabbing I admit but back then I was just this hyper wild LITTLE BOY really, big for my age maybe but not *that* big. It was just this weird MYSTERY, all of them, all their reasons—Let's do what's BEST FOR MICKEY everybody and it felt like jail, like waking up in solitary. I mean it wasn't like I loved my parents but I thought I was supposed to and they shoved me off man, they sent me off in the old lifeboat.

Was like they could always say to themselves well we didn't GET him until he was four years old, he's got things in him we didn't put there—my mother told me once I had probably been abused as a young kid which is maybe likely because from the first I knew I was full of hate, just HATE, hate, a little jet-propelled demon. You think I'm abrasive now—wasn't that the word, Mickey's new word from the lady with the big vocabulary?—yeah, *abrasive,* you should have seen me *then.* I did it with dedication, like something was boiling over a fire inside me, you know? I don't have any memory before about age six. No, I DON'T remember any real parents. I mean, my mother is Jewish and my father is Quaker, and they can't have any more kids so they decide to adopt two Indians. Yeah, the liberal American melting pot and what it melted was my head. But that's OK, I dig being runny and hot, I just don't ever want to be dead and I don't give a shit what anyone thinks because I'm not amusing YOU you see I'm amusing MYSELF and whoever digs THAT can stand on my train. I got myself strapped to a big diesel and I got no complaints. I got a lot to do and I'm really HERE, they can all tell and that's why I'm going to make it. I got talent, I got total energy and focus and I can hold a stage. You've never even seen me sing and you can feel it. Just ice, ice and hot white sparks, squeeze it out and control what they feel. It's not how fucking OLD I am or cocktail manners or social skills, it's what I know and no one TAKES that, I GIVE it, *I* give it.

I could always take care of myself, all us kids could, because my mother was sick so much of the time. She has lupus, always had it for years, that's why I'm back here from England now. She's not well, she's not at all well. But we kids did our own shit, I mean we washed our own clothes and cleaned up after ourselves and cooked the fucking meals, yeah, casseroles, but still, Mickey is no slouch in the kitchen—that's why it's so funny to me to see these guys who can't wipe their own asses, fucking helpless without a girl to sew their buttons on. I mean that's not what I need a girl for, you know? And the food thing, I always worked in restaurants, those jobs are easy to get and bartending pays if you hang around long enough to get the good shifts. I was doing fifty a night when you met me and don't worry I'll do it again, but Savio's man, is the craziest place in the Square, all the nuts are in there, the regulars, every night near closing—like that old lady you saw that tried to throw her glass at me. She's in there, sitting on the barstool and talking to herself until she works up a fury. Turns to the other customers with this blitz of curses about whoever serves her DID YOU SEE WHAT HE SAID TO ME THAT UGLY MONKEY LOOK AT HIM PUSHING HIS WHITE TEETH OUT JESUS CHRIST I DON'T HAVE TO TAKE THIS SHIT HE'S AN APE AN APE MAN A STUPID BABOON. Finally you ask her if she has the money to pay her bill and she never does, three times the manager had to help her off the stool and into the street and she's yelling all the way about how I'd slapped her in the face and ripped her dress. Then there's Veteran Twitch, this wipe-out in army fatigues who's always there at closing, totally gonzo but very quiet, stares into his glass and does this endless routine of facial expressions, wound up tight and talking nonstop with no sound. Never raises his eyes but definitely directs it all to some companion on the phantom telephone. You don't know how many nuts there are till you work a bar, I only do it because they don't lay claims, you do it and get out. And I save all the bucks, I got back from England and was at my parents' house, couldn't handle it so I was renting this studio, a sound studio so I could get some musicians together and do some tapes, $350 a month, that's where all my money went and I'm sneaking in there at night and sleeping as well and it was useless as far as the music went, I just couldn't find anyone who was serious, they're on their way to law school and born cool, they got to make the Cotillion in their MGs. The music ain't going to come from THEM it's going to come from ME because it's all I GOT, and then I'm gonna be laughing in their faces which is maybe a pointless desire because by the time I get there their faces will have long since been turned to the wall, staring at nowhere, nothing every minute.

Talk about walls, the rules can do it and women can do it too, put you on your back unexpectedly. Rules do it over the long haul so you don't even notice but girls can do it with one punch, like Giselle, the girl I lived with here between the two times I was in England. Giselle was a beautiful little girl, man I will always love her but she was crazy and her life had been shit. She was from the Projects in South Boston and she talked with that nasal flat twang and was all fashion, living at home with her fucking drunk father and her drunk brothers and spending all her money from her boring job on shiny shoes and satin jackets. She was twenty-one and I was eighteen and I took her out of there like Prince Valiant, had a good bar job and a place in Allston. Giselle was blond, real petite, maybe 5′2″—I like small girls anyway, so nice and light to lift and hold in bed—but Giselle had such a way of *standing,* like a kid with her hands empty. You wouldn't think much of her, I mean she had nothing to say really, she wasn't so much for brains if you judge by talk, but she had so much heart and would just look at you with everything laid open, like there was nothing she wouldn't give you. Jesus, Giselle—she got to me, I lived with her the longest, about six months, but she had to possess you, surround you. She was a big help to me and I got a lot of work done then on my music, I lost a waiting job during that time and she took over with the money, but later I got a bar thing together and was meeting a lot of ladies. I couldn't lie to her so we broke up and she moved back home. I would still go to see her there though I hated that apartment building, all dark and stale with the TVs going. I called her at work one day to see how she was, I knew she was hassled about me, and they told me she'd been sent home drunk from lunch. Really wasn't like her to fuck up a job. So I went by to see her and I find her in her bedroom really juiced and weepy, the room a mess, she could barely talk. I stayed there with her about two hours but then I had to leave to meet Janet, this other girl I was going out with—and Giselle just grabs on to me, begs me not to go, stay, stay with me. I told her I had to split but she could come, I figured I'd take her back to my place and let her sleep it off. But she said no, I had to stay *there* in her bedroom and not move until she was all right. So I'm walking toward the door and she's following, yelling how she's going to kill herself. We're on this falling-down stoop in the Projects and she's screaming and I told her not to be stupid, don't be crazy, and she slammed the door in my face. I went off to meet Janet but I was worried, I remembered Giselle's girl friend telling me how Giselle had tried to kill herself once before over a guy. Tried to phone her but no one home. So that night about three A.M. Janet and I are asleep in my apartment and this tornado blows through the door— Boom Boom Boom—I hear three giant steps as Giselle makes the distance from the door to the bed and then banshee screaming YOU FUCKER I KNEW YOU HAD SOMEONE HERE and fists and I rolled over Janet first to protect her and grabbed Giselle's wrists. I couldn't hold her, she was totally out of her head, kicking and punching me, she kicked me in the balls about three times and bloodied my face. This went on for about twenty full-blown minutes, and then she seemed to calm down and said she was going into the kitchen to wash up. So I'm wiping the blood off my mouth, *tired* man, exhausted, from fighting this tiny girl, and in shock from falling into it out of a total sleep. I mean, I didn't even know she still had a key—she'd given it back a month before when she'd moved out but made a copy on the sly. I found out later she'd been coming over to the place when I wasn't there and just sitting in the rooms, for hours. Anyway, I'm standing there and Giselle walks back in with a butcher knife. She has it in both hands above her head and she's bringing it down into her own stomach and I lunged across the room and grabbed her—she cut my chest and kept trying to stab me. I couldn't get the knife out of her hands. I yelled to Janet to call the police but I had unplugged the phone earlier and Janet couldn't find the socket to plug it back in, so I'm dragging Giselle around by the arms to show Janet where the phone plug is, blood dripping down my legs from the cuts—really getting scared because this thing doesn't ever seem to be ending, Janet with her clothes on by now and panic-stricken and Giselle like a frozen monster and all three of us crying—I couldn't see anything for crying. It was a nightmare, like getting caught in fast water and you can't tell what's happening, you're just getting beaten from every direction and going under. Janet got the police but there was more blood from somewhere and it really flashed through my mind that Giselle might kill me—it took the fucking cops fifteen minutes to get there and by the time they did I was lying on top of Giselle on the floor, naked and bleeding on both of us, holding her down with my weight and the knife still in her fist. As soon as I got off her she was up and throwing a tape recorder she'd given me through the window, then she picked up a chair—not a great big chair but this was a tiny girl. The cops put her in a straitjacket and when she came to herself she was behind bars, clutching this

little suitcase she'd brought over to my place with her.
I called a friend of mine to go down and get her out
of jail and tell the cops it was domestic and no charges
and all that crap, and she went to her girl friend's and
soon after left for Mexico—this trip we'd planned for
her when she was still living with me. We'd gotten the
air tickets and everything and talked about how getting away would make the transition easier for her.
Jesus. This was all about a year and a half ago now and
Giselle seems OK, living with some guy who goes
home to her every night and lets her cook his dinner.
I still care about her, I can't forget the good things
about her, but I don't go to sleep now without a chain
lock across the door. That was the scariest thing that
ever happened to me, and the worst of it was seeing
her in that straitjacket. Have you ever seen someone
you know in one? She looked amputated, lopped off
and exploding, her arms *gone* when I'd felt them *holding* me all that time before.

Holding is a trip, right? The last time my mother was
in the hospital, I stayed up with her all one night and
couldn't get my head clear for days afterward. She was
on chemotherapy then, some drug that was mostly
speed because she couldn't sleep at all, and she had
these speed raps with everyone in the family. All of us,
one at a time, late at night. I'm alone with her in that
room, she's the only one of them I love. She told me
how hard it was to raise me—I said, shit, you didn't
raise me, from the age of twelve I was a ward of the
State, you call that *raising* me, I mean I was bounced
around like a fucking ball and you so-called parents
didn't pay for nothing, my clothes, my lodging, my
schooling, *nothing*—and no one says you *had* to but
then to get on my ass about owing you fifteen bucks,
FIFTEEN BUCKS man. Blame me for that if you want
to, she says, I'm only trying to teach you to care about

someone's rules but your own, and we had to let you go Mickey, you were tearing us up, you were tearing all of us apart, it was you or all the rest of them, I had to decide. Why did you hate us, she says, Why Did You Hate All Of Us coming at me pounding in my head like a drum, Christ, in that dark hospital, the halls dark and the nurses squeaking shoes outside. My legs were shaking, I wanted to get up and run but I couldn't stand up, just her FACE in that bed man— I took her face between my two hands and I YELLED right at her EYES, I didn't hate YOU I hated THEM, I LOVED YOU. Fucking Christ. Now she's home. She's home now and I'm gone, I can't go over there. If I weren't staying with you I'd be staying somewhere else.

All you can do is turn the bad stuff into something else and not flake out on what it costs you—like, I know I'm good, I got metal and breath in my voice and I can hold any space. Use a voice like playing a horn, peeling and slow whines and a good bass—like, *I'M FLYin on an AIRPLANE / I'M WALKin on a LAKE / MOVE my LIFE AROUND / BUT IT'S ALL A MISTAKE*—hard undercut in the bass, that flat BWAA BOOM in the lyrics lays down a gut tremor they can't help but give you, give BACK to you. *An DON'T YOU WISH / somebody knew you / an DON'T YOU DREAM / somebody calls your name*—Yeah, I know I've got it, I sing in the streets and I can hear people pick it up behind me. I'm back in Europe just as soon as I get the bread, there's no rock clubs here, nowhere to do a good band, just posers man, just wearing the fancy leather and the chains and stepping out to masquerade, barns full of sweaty dress-ups, all MONEY, they all got money and no pressure, no push—they don't know shit about music but it doesn't even MATTER man, the ones doing real music can do it without them and just play

them, play them like mongoloid pinball—Nothin fucks
music, what it *has,* melts in your mouth and turns to
acid halfway down, you don't forget it. AM slosh is no
real language. Look, you feel my mouth, you see,
we're talking.

Here, I want to keep my face close to your face. You
share your pillows with me, OK darling? I'll be YOUR
friend.

When it gets to be night like this, I mean late night—
night doesn't start till three A.M.—I like how there's no
light and the dark is different from earlier, when
they're all out there checking scenes and looking for
some flash. About now everyone starts sinking. . . .
What do you think? we're not bad roommates—Darling, put those cards away, don't play games in bed.
What? You can tell my fortune with those cards? I
believe in that shit, don't scare me . . . turn out the
light, I got something for you, do it in the dark if
you're going to do it . . .

RAYME

*I*n our student days we were all in need of fortune tellers. No one was sure what was happening in the outside world and no one thought about it much. We had no televisions and we bought few newspapers. Communal life seemed a continual dance in which everyone changed partners, a patient attempt at domesticity by children taking turns being parents. We were adrift but we were together. A group of us floated among several large ramshackle houses, houses arranged above and below each other on steep streets: a gritty version of terraced dwellings in some exotic Asia. The houses were old and comfortable, furnished with an accumulation of overstuffed chairs and velveteen sofas gleaned from rummage sales. There were no curtains on the large windows, whose rectangular sooty light was interrupted only by tangles of viny plants. The plants were fed haphazardly and thrived, like anything green in that town, enveloping sills and frames still fitted with the original wavy glass of seventy years before. The old glass was pocked with flaws and minute bubbles, distorting further the vision of a town already oddly displaced and dreamed in jagged pieces. Houses of the student ghetto were the landscape of the dream— a landscape often already condemned.

I lived in a house on Price Street with three male housemates: a Lebanese photographer from Rochester, New York, a Jewish TM instructor from Michigan, and a carpenter musician, a West Virginian, who'd worked in the doomed McCarthy campaign and dropped out of Harvard Law to come home and learn housebuilding.

This story could be about any one of those people, but it is about Rayme and comes to no conclusions.

Perhaps the story is about Rayme because she lived in all the communal houses at one time or another. Intermittently she lived with her father and stepmother and brother. Or she lived with one of her two older sisters, who had stayed in town and were part of our group of friends. Or she lived in her own small rooms, a bedroom, kitchen, and bath in a house chopped into three or four such apartments. She lived alone in several of those single-person places, and in all of them she kept the provided mattress and box springs tilted upright against the wall. She slept on a small rug that she unrolled at night, or she slept on the bare floor with the rug precisely folded as a pillow. She shoved most of the other furniture into a corner or put it outside on the porch. Skirts and coats on hangers, swatches of fabric, adorned the walls. Rayme brought in large branches, a brick, a rock. Usually there were no utilities but running water; her father paid the rent and that is all that was paid. She wore sweaters and leggings and burned candles for light. She used the refrigerator as a closet for shoes and beads, and seemed to eat almost nothing. She kept loose tea and seeds in jars and emptied coffee cans that she filled with nutshells and marbles. A long time ago her mother had committed suicide in Argentina. No one ever talked about the death, but one of Rayme's sisters told me the suicide was slow rather than overtly violent. "She stopped eating, she'd been sick, she wouldn't go to the hospital or see a doctor," the sister said. "It took her several months to do it." Rayme seldom mentioned her mother and didn't seem certain of any particular chain of events concerning the past. The facts she referred to at different times seemed arbitrary, they were scrambled, they may have been false or transformed. It is true that her parents married each other twice and divorced twice; the father was a professor, the mother had musical talent and four children. Rayme told me her father wouldn't let his wife play the piano; he locked the baby grand because she became too "detached" when she played.

The first time her parents divorced, Rayme was six years old, the only child to go with her mother. They lived alone together in Kansas. Rayme didn't remember much about it. She said sometimes she came home from school and the door would be locked and she would sit outside past dark and listen to the owls in the trees. Once there was a tornado in Kansas; Rayme's mother opened all the windows "so the wind can blow *through* the house instead of breaking it." Then they sat on the sofa wrapped in their winter coats, rather than hiding in the basement, so they could watch the rattling funnel cloud twist and hop across the flat fields behind the town.

Rayme said her mother kept things in Kansas, like bracelets and rings, costume jewelry, under the pillows of the bed. They used to play games with those things before they went to sleep at night, and tell stories. Rayme slept by the wall because her mother sleepwalked and needed a clear path to the open.

At the time of the second divorce, Rayme was twelve. She said her father stood in the middle of the living room and called out the names of the children. He pointed to one side of the room or the other. "When we were lined up right, he said *those* kids would stay with him and *those* kids would go with her." Rayme went to Argentina with her mother and oldest sister. A family friend there paid airplane fares and found housing; Rayme's father paid child support. Rayme learned some Spanish songs. Her sister went out on chaperoned dates, there was a terrace, it was sunny. Their mother died down there after a few months, and the two children came back on a boat, unchaperoned.

Rayme's sister told me Rayme didn't react when their mother died. "Everyone else cried, but Rayme didn't. She just sat there on the bed. She was our mother's favorite." The funeral was in Argentina, and the service was Catholic. "I was standing by the door while the priest was in the bedroom," Rayme's sister said. "Rayme looked up at me wearing our mother's expression, on purpose, to say *I'd* lost my mother but *she* hadn't."

Once Rayme sent her oldest sister a group of wallet-sized photographs in the mail. They were all pictures of Rayme taken in various years by public school photographers, and they were all dotted with tiny pinholes so that the faces were gone. Another time she came to her sister's Christmas party with one eyebrow shaved off. Her sister demanded that she shave the other one off as well so at least they'd match, and Rayme did.

Sometime late that winter, Rayme went to stay in the country at the cabin of a friend. She was living there alone with her cat; she said she could marry the snow. The cat wandered into the woods and Rayme wandered down the middle of the dirt road six miles to the highway. There was rain and a heavy frost, sleet flowers on the pavement. Rayme wore a summer shift and a kitchen knife strapped to her arm with leather thongs. She had hacked her waist-length hair to the shape of a bowl on her head and coiled her thick dark braids tightly into the pockets of her dress.

She had nothing to say to the farm couple who found her sitting on the double line of the highway in a meditative pose, but she did nod and get into the car as though expecting them. They took her to the university hospital and she committed herself for three weeks. I visited her there; she sat stiffly by a window reinforced with chicken wire between double panes, her back very straight, her hands clasped. She said it was important to practice good posture, and she moved her head, slowly, deliberately, when she looked to the right or left. Her skin was pale and clear like white porcelain. Before I left, we repeated some rituals evolved earlier in half-serious fun: children's songs with hand motions ("here is the church and here is the steeple" . . . "I'm a little teapot, short and stout" . . . "along came the rain and washed the spider out"), the Repulse Tiger movement from T'ai Chi, a series of Chinese bows in slow motion. She said the hospital was like a big clock and she was in the floor of the clock; every day she went to Group, and played dominoes in the Common Room. She ate her lunch in a chair by the nurses' desk; she liked their white clothes and the sighing of the elevators.

By the time she was released, the TM instructor

living at Price Street had moved to Cleveland. Rayme moved in with me, with the Harvard carpenter, with the Lebanese photographer. She wasn't paying rent but we had the extra room anyway and sometimes she cooked meals.

Once she cooked soup. For an hour, she stood by the stove, stirring the soup in a large dented kettle. I looked into the pot and saw a jagged object floating among the vegetables. I pulled it out, holding the hot, thin edge: it was a large fragment of blackened linoleum from the buckling kitchen floor.

I asked Rayme how a piece of the floor got into the soup.

"I put it there," Rayme said.

I didn't answer.

"It's clean," Rayme said, "I washed it first," and then, angrily, "If you're not going to eat my food, don't look at it."

That was her worst summer. She told me she didn't want to take the Thorazine because it made her into someone else. Men were the sky and women were the earth; she liked books about Indians. She said cats were good and dogs were bad; she hated the lower half of her body. She didn't have lovers but quietly adored men from her past—relatives, boyfriends, men she saw in magazines or on the street. Her high school boyfriend was Krishna, a later one Jesus, her father "Buddha with a black heart." She built an altar in her room out of planks and cement blocks, burned candles and incense, arranged pine needles and pebbles in patterns. She changed costumes often and moved the furniture in her room several times a day, usually shifting it just a few inches. She taped pictures on her wall: blue Krishna riding his white pony, Shiva dancing with all her gold arms adorned, Lyndon Johnson in glossy color from *Newsweek*, cutouts of kittens from a toilet-paper advertisement. Her brother, three years younger than she and just graduated from high school, came to see her several times a week. He brought her a blue bottle full of crushed mint, and played his guitar. He seemed quiet, witty, focused; he looked like Rayme, the same dark hair and slender frame and chiseled bones. She said he was the angel who flew from the window with sleep-dust on his shoes; he used to tell his sisters, when they were all children, that he was the one who'd sealed their eyes shut in the night, that they would never catch him because boys could be ghosts in the dark.

On an afternoon when we'd taken mescaline, Rayme sat weeping on the couch at Price Street. The couch was brown and nubby, and people had to sit toward its edge or the cushions would fall through to the floor. The cushions had fallen through, and Rayme sat in the hole of the frame comfortably, her legs splayed up over the board front. She sat looking at the ceiling, her head thrown back, like a woman trying to keep her mascara from running. She remained still, as though enthroned, waiting, her face wet, attentive. I watched her from across the room. "Yes," she said after a long while, as though apprehending some truth, "tears wash the eyes and lubricate the skin of the temples."

All of us were consulting a series of maps bearing no relation to any physical geography, and Rayme was like a telephone to another world. Her messages were syllables from an investigative dream, and her every movement was precise, like those of a driver unerringly steering an automobile by watching the road through the rearview mirror.

I'd met her when we were both working at Bonanza Steak House as servers. She liked the cowboy hats and the plaid shirts with the braid trim, and she insisted on completing the outfit by wearing her brother's high-heeled boots and a string tie from Carlsbad Caverns emblazoned with a tiny six-gun. She got away with these embellishments of store policy because her compulsions seemed harmless. She would stand erect behind plates of crackling steaks bound for numbered trays, looking intently into the vacuous faces of customers shuffling by in the line. She did tap-dance steps in place, wielding her spatula and tipping her hat, addressing everyone as Sir or Madam. She liked the ritual of the totally useless weekly employee meetings, in which skirt lengths and hairnets and customer quotas were discussed. She admired the manager and called him Mr. Fenstermaker, when everyone else referred to him derisively as "Chester," after the gimp on "Gunsmoke." He was a fat doughy boy about thirty years old who walked around what he called "the store" with a clipboard of names and work hours. During meetings Rayme sat at his elbow and took down his directives in careful, cursive script, posting them later on the door to the employees' bathroom. She also posted the covers of several romance comic books. She got in trouble once for mixing the mashed potatoes with nutmeg and banana slices, and again when she arranged the plastic steak tags across the raw meat in a mandala bordered by white stones. In the center of the mandala was the small, perfect egg of a bird. The egg was purely blue; on it Rayme had painted a Chinese word in miniature gold characters. Later she told me she'd looked the word up especially in a language textbook; the word meant "banquet."

Rayme was protected at Price Street. She stopped losing jobs because she stopped having them; instead, she worked in the tumbledown garden, tying tomato plants to poles with strips of heavy satin and brocade —draperies she'd found in a junk pile. Meticulously, she cut the fabric into measured lengths and hemmed the pieces. She kept the house full of wild flowers and blossoming weeds, and hung herbs to dry in the hallways. The summer was easy. No one expected her to talk on days when she didn't speak. She was calm. She pretended we were mythical people and brought us presents she'd made: a doll of sticks and corn silk, with a shard of glass for a face, or the skeleton of a lizard laid out perfectly in a velvet-lined harmonica box.

In late August we were told that Price Street and the abandoned houses near it would be demolished by the city, "to make the city hospital a more attractive property." The rest of us complained resignedly but Rayme made no comment; quietly, she began staying awake all night in the downstairs of the house. Day after day, we awoke to find the furniture turned over and piled in a heap, the rugs rolled up, pictures turned upside down on the walls. She took personal possessions from the bedrooms, wrapped them in her shirts and jeans, and tied the carefully folded parcels with twine. We called a house meeting to discuss her behavior, and Rayme refused to attend. She went upstairs and began throwing plates from the windows.

We asked her brother to come to Price Street and talk to her. They sat in her room for a couple of hours, then they came downstairs. Rayme said she didn't have any money, maybe she'd live with her sister for a while. She unwrapped the stolen possessions with great ceremony and gave them back to us as gifts while her brother watched, smiling. At midnight, we made wheat pancakes and ate them with molasses, Indian-style, on the dark porch.

Several years later, when all the houses we'd lived in together had been torn down, Rayme's brother would shoot himself with a pistol. He would do it beside a lean-to he'd built as a squatter at an isolated campsite, five miles up a steep mountain trail. He would leave no notes; his body would not be discovered for some time. When they did find him ("they" meaning people in uniforms), they would have trouble getting a stretcher down the path and over the rocks.

But this was before that. It was September of 1974, most of us would leave town in a few weeks, and I had been recently pregnant. Some of us were going to Belize to survive an earthquake. Some of us were going to California to live on 164th Street in Oakland. A few were staying in West Virginia to continue the same story in even more fragmented fashion. My lover, the carpenter, was going to Nicaragua on a house-building deal that would never materialize. We'd had passport photos taken together; he would use his passport in the company of someone else and I would lose mine somewhere in Arizona. But on this day in September I had never seen Arizona, and we all went to a deserted lake to swim despite the fact the weather had turned.

I remember going into the lake first, how the water was warmer than the air. On the bank the others were taking off their clothes—denim skirts and jeans, soft, worn clothes, endlessly utilitarian. Their bodies were pale and slow against the dark border of the woods. They walked into the lake separately, aimlessly, but Rayme swam straight toward me. It was almost evening and the air smelled of rain. Noise was muffled by the wind in the leaves of the trees, and when Rayme was suddenly close the splash of her movement was a shock like waking up. Her hands brushed my legs— her touch underwater as soft as the touch of a plant— and she passed me, swimming deeper, swimming farther out.

I wanted to stand on something firm and swam to the dock, a stationary thickness for mooring motorboats. It stretched out into the water a long distance. Who had built it in this deserted place? It was old, the weathered black of railroad ties. I pulled myself onto the splintery wood and began to walk along its length, touching the pylons, hearing the *swak* of stirred water as the storm blew up, hearing my own footsteps. Where were we all really going, and when would we ever arrive? Our destinations appeared to be inter-changeable pauses in some long, lyric transit. This time that was nearly over, these years, seemed as close to family as most of us would ever get.

Now the rain was coming from far off, sweeping across the water in a silver sheet. The waiting surface began to dapple, studded with slivers of rain. Rayme was a white face and shoulders, afloat two hundred yards out. "Kate," she called across the distance, "when you had your abortion, did you think about killing yourself?"

"No," I yelled back. "Come out of the water."

FAST LANES

Colorado, 1975

We walked down
a grassy knoll to the lake.

"The truck should be OK there," he said. "Place is
deserted."

Behind us the pickup sat squat and red in the sun,
a black tarp roped across the boxes and trunks in the
bed. Hot and slick, the tarp shimmered like a dark
liquid. The rest stop was a small gravel lot marked by
a low wooden fence and three large aluminum trash
cans chained to posts. Beyond it the access road, un-
lined and perfectly smooth, glittered in a slant of heat.

"Where are we?" I asked.

"Somewhere in west Georgia."

I could close my eyes and still feel myself across the seat of the moving truck, my head on his sour thigh and my knees tucked up. The steering wheel was a curved black bar close to my face, its dark grooves turning. We hadn't spoken since pulling out of the motel parking lot in New Orleans. Now I stumbled and he drew me up beside him. The weeds were thick and silky. Pollen rose in clouds and settled in the haze. The incline grew steeper and we seemed to slide into the depths of the grass, then the ground leveled and several full elms banded the water. The bank was green to its edge. We entered the shade of the trees and felt the coolness through our shoes. He stepped out of his unlaced sneakers, pulled off his shirt and jeans. The belt buckle clanked on stones. Then he stood, touching the white skin of his stomach. His eyes were blue as blue glass, and bloodshot. He hadn't slept.

"You all right?" he said.

I didn't answer.

"You've got no obligation to me," he said. "I don't tell you who to pick up in a bar. But at eight o'clock this morning I began to wonder if I was going to have to leave you, and dump all that crap of yours in the middle of Bourbon Street."

He turned, moving through high grass to the water. I saw him step in and push out, sinking to his shoulders. "Thurman," I said, but he was under, weaving long and pale below the surface.

I took off my dress and let it fall into the grass white and wrinkled, smelling of rum. The lake seemed to grow as I got closer, yawning like a cool mouth at the center of the heat. I was in it; I sank to my knees as water closed over me, then felt the settling mud as I lay flat and tried to stay down. I held my knees and swayed, hearing nothing. Their faces were fading, and the lines of white coke across the gleaming desk top.

I rolled to my side and the water pushed, darkening, purple. It was Thurman, moving closer, changing the colors, and I felt his hands on my arms. He pulled me up and the air cracked as we surfaced, streaming water.

I wasn't crying but I felt the leaden air move out of my chest. I felt how hard he was holding me and knew I was shaking. My heart beat in my throat and ears, pounding. He held my heavy hair pulled back and bunched in one hand, and with the other he poured water down my neck and shoulders, stroking with the warmth of his palm in the coolness. He said low disconnected words, mother sounds and lullabies. I felt my teeth in my lips and my forehead moving slowly against his chest. Holding to his big shoulders, I could feel him with all my body.

"I drew a map to the motel on that napkin and you lost it, didn't you," he said. "I knew you would. We were both drunk when I gave it to you."

Behind his voice there was a hum of insects and locusts and the faraway sound of the highway. The highway played three chords beyond his reddened arms; a low thrum, a continual median sigh, and a whine so shrill it was gone as it started. The sounds separated and converged, like the sounds of their voices in the room last night and the driftings of music from the club below. There was a discreet jarring of dishes or silver at a long distance, and the sound of the bed, close, under me, but fake, like a sound through a wall that might after all be a recording, someone's joke.

I was talking then, because Thurman said, "No, no joke." As he said it I could feel the water again, around us, between us.

"I lose track of where I am," I said.

"Stand still. You're OK now. No one's trying anything. It's me. Remember me? The driver?"

"Yeah. I remember you. You're the one born in Dallas."

"Right. That's good. Now listen. We're going to walk out of the water and dry off for five minutes. I'm not going to touch you. You'll feel fine in the sun and I'll smoke a joint." He turned in the water, holding my wrist, pulling me gently toward the shore.

"I can't put that dress on again," I said.

"Then leave it for the next refugee. Leave it where it is."

"No one should wear it."

"You can wear my shirt," he said. "You'll look great in blue denim and no pants, like Doris Day in a pajama movie."

Thurman had seen a lot of Doris Day movies in Dallas, in neighborhood theaters that weren't the Ritz. His two older brothers kissed girls in the balcony while he sat in the back row downstairs with the Mexicans. Blue-eyed Doris flickered in a bad print to the tune of bubbly music and wetback jeers. Thurman said he liked Doris in those days because she was so out-of-it she made no sense to anyone, and she kept right on raising her eyebrows, perky, not quite smart, as wads of paper and popcorn boxes bounced off the screen. Afterward he walked home with his brothers across the freeway, up long sidewalks to what was just a few houses then, not yet a suburb. His brothers told tales on the girls and teased him about sitting with the Mexicans. At home they sometimes shook him by his heels over the toilet, flushed it, and threatened to drop him in. That, said Thurman, was a precursor to all of Dallas in the '50s and early '60s: fringed shirts, steaming sidewalk grates globbed with saliva in the summer, first-time gang bangs in a whorehouse with steers' heads on the walls. Not just the horns, he said, the whole fucking head, stuffed, like it was a lion from

Africa. And football, always football; Thurman's father was a successful high school coach who took pride in featuring his own sons on his teams. One after another, he'd coached, punished, driven them all to a grueling and temporary stardom.

When I met Thurman he was floating and I was floating home. He drove a Datsun pickup and he lived in the foothills near Denver. He had a small wooden house with a slanted kitchen, a broken water heater, and a new skylight framed in white pine against old ceiling boards and dangling strips of flowered wallpaper. He played music with friends of mine and did carpentry and called me up once to eat with him at a good Indian restaurant. He'd been in the Peace Corps in Ceylon and he said you should eat this food right out of the bowls with your hand, but only one hand. The other stayed in your lap to prove you used separate hands for eating and for cleaning yourself.

He stayed with me that night, mostly because I liked the way he looked from the back as he bought oranges later, threading his way through the panhandlers at an open air market. He had a cloth bag swinging at his hip but none of them asked for change. He was big and broad-shouldered in a blousy white shirt, redheaded and ruddy; he'd gotten slightly dressed up and called me without really knowing me to pretend a good dinner was no big deal. He was probably lonely, but he moved nicely, mannish, not arrogant, tossing the oranges into a bag with the casual finesse of an ex-athlete still in shape at thirty. The sun was going down; it was early summer; the fruit was stacked in green trays like pretty ornaments. I didn't really want Thurman but I liked him and it was time to sleep with someone. I knew he'd be patient and slow and if I got a little high it would be OK, I'd feel better. But we went on too long, he woke me again in the night, and the next morning he wanted to stay around. He'd lived with someone quite a while in San Antonio; it had broken up three years before, but he still dated history from that time: all the towns he'd lived in since, Berkeley, Austin, Jackson, Eugene, Denver, all the western floater's towns. We talked about money—how I'd spent mine having mono I'd caught waitressing and eating off plates, how he was making a lot building houses in the mountains with a crew of dealers from Aspen. Finally he drank his orange juice and left. I didn't think of him much until a month later when I read his notice advertising for riders on a bookstore bulletin board. He was taking off for a while, down through Texas and Louisiana, then up the coast. I went looking and found him installing wooden doors on a cold-storage cabinet at a natural foods store.

"You leaving for good?" he asked. "Going home?"

"Leaving here for good. I won't stay home long."

"Then why go? For the hell of it?"

"It's a long story, Thurman. I'd rather not go into it here by the plum nectar and the juice cartons advertising Enlightenment."

"You're a cynic," he said, measuring the blond frame of the door. "That's why you're leaving. You can't take it here in Paradise where everyone is beautiful and girls aren't allowed to wear makeup."

"You've got it. I want to go back to my hometown and buy mascara."

"You wouldn't be caught dead in mascara." He lifted the piece of glass against the frame, checking the fit, then set it down again. Looking at me through the open door of the cabinet, he held the lock in one hand and rummaged in his apron for screws. "I accept you as my rider."

I looked at the floor, then back up at him. "The thing is, I need to get there pretty quickly. My father is sick."

"How sick?"

"Just sick. He has to have an operation in two or three weeks."

"Well," he said, and ran his hand along the wood, "you'd almost get there in time. Three weeks would be the best I could do. Stopovers on the way. But you won't have to worry about money. Just pay for your food." He looked away from me, leaning back to fit the lock. "Is it a deal?"

"It's the best deal I've got."

"Good. I'm leaving in four days."

"Thurman," I said, "is this a kissy-poo number?"

He tested the hinges and shrugged. "It's no particular number. Whatever works out. Besides, you can handle me. I'm a pushover."

"Fine. I'm going home to pack."

I turned and walked out, and as I hit the street I heard him yelling behind me, "Listen, can you sing with the radio? Can you carry a tune?"

We pulled out of town at dawn. I had the feeling, the floater's only fix: I was free, it didn't matter if I never saw these streets again; even as we passed them they receded and entered a realm of placeless streets. Even the people were gone, the good ones and the bad ones; I owned whatever real had occurred, I took it all. I was vanished, invisible, another apartment left empty behind me, my possessions given away, thrown away, packed away in taped boxes fit into an available vehicle. The vehicle was the light, the early light and later the darkness.

"Hey dreamer," Thurman said, "what are you doing?"

"Praying," I said.

He smiled. "I did some speed, I'm going to just keep going. Sleep when you want to."

"OK," I said.

"New Mexico, tomorrow morning."

"Good. That will be pretty."

Thurman drove straight to an all-night stop in Albuquerque, the apartment of a stewardess he'd known in college. It was the first floor of a complex right off the freeway, motel terraces and a Naugahyde couch. She was gone and it seemed she'd never been there, empty shelves and pebbly white walls with no marks. I sat up in bed while my legs still shook from holding him.

"You could be such a good lover," he said. "I can feel you have been, but you're so busy stepping out."

"This mattress is too soft." I moved away from him. "The sheets feel heavy. I'm going to sleep in the other room on the floor."

"The floor," he said. He lit a cigarette. "It's a shame you can't levitate, so that even the floor couldn't touch you."

I went into the living room and pushed the furniture against the walls. There were only three pieces: the black couch and chair and a Formica table. They all seemed weightless, like cardboard. I lay down in the middle of the carpeted floor with my arms out and my feet together, counting each breath, counting with the hum of the air-conditioner. I went away. I heard nothing until I felt him in the room. He was sitting beside me, cross-legged, in the dark.

"What are you scared of?" he said.

"I don't know. Going back."

"Explain. Tell Thurman."

"I can't. Sometimes it's hard to breathe, like living under blankets."

"Hot?"

"Hot, but cold too. Shaking."

"Then don't go back."

"I have to," I said. "It doesn't help anymore to stay away."

He stood up and went to the bedroom. I heard him pull the sheet off the bed in one motion, the sheet coming clear with a soft snap. He brought a pillow too, stood at my feet, and furled the white sheet out so it settled over me like the rectangular flag of some pure and empty country.

"It's midnight," he said. "Get some sleep. We need to be out of here early."

By nine A.M. we were two hours south of the city on Rte. 25. We didn't talk; the road was a straight two-lane, the light still clear but thickening with heat to come later. Both of us had wanted out of that apartment by dawn; we'd drank a half-carton of orange juice we'd found in the spotless refrigerator, drank it as we pulled out of the parking lot, shrouded in a half-stupor of fatigue. Thurman held the wheel steady with one knee, staring ahead. "Can you drive a standard shift?"

"Maybe," I said, "except I haven't for a while. I'm not sure I still know how."

"What?" His voice was flat. "You're twenty-three and American and you can't drive?"

"I have a license. Just never used it."

"Why not?"

"Because when I was sixteen I pulled into the driveway in my mother's car, sideswiped my father's car, and rear-ended my brother's car."

Thurman shook his head. "Wonderful."

"I was only going ten miles an hour—there wasn't much damage. Scratches and dented chrome. But afterward my driving was a family joke and no one would let me behind the wheel."

"I can imagine."

"Besides, it was a small town. My boyfriends had cars."

"Well," he said, "this is no small town and there's no boyfriend in sight. You're going to learn how to drive."

"Thurman, are you going to liberate me?"

"No, you're going to liberate me. I plan to spend exactly half this trip pleasantly stoned, playing with the radio and reading girlie magazines."

"I didn't know you read girlie magazines."

"Only the really sleazy ones, the ones with no pretensions. And I don't want any shit about it."

He pulled off the road near Cuchillo and took a left off the exit. We could see the town in the distance, brown and white and hunched. Thurman drove in the opposite direction. The land was absolutely flat, wavering with heat, a moony unreal surface even as mirrors. Light glanced off like knife glare. The far mountains were blue and beige, treeless. "Pinos Altos," Thurman said, "or the Mimbres range, I don't know which. We aren't far from Elephant Butte and the reservation." He steered onto the berm of the narrow road, slowed and stopped as yellow dust rose around us. "Good spot for a ceremony." He turned off the ignition and faced me. He seemed amazingly defined in that early, hot light, a film of moisture on his forehead, his big hands opening toward me in even gestures, describing small spheres as he talked.

"Now," he said, "this is going to take twenty minutes. Remember, a standard is always the best transmission—it allows you to feel the machine and the road more efficiently than an automatic. Nobody who knows much about cars drives an automatic."

"Automatics are for cherries, right, Thurman?"

He got out of the truck and stood looking in at me from the road. "Slide over."

"Do we have to be so serious? It was a joke."

"I'm not laughing. In thirty minutes this pleasant eighty-degree interlude will be over and the temperature will be climbing right up to about a hundred and ten. It's early September in Texas. We will need to be moving. So pay attention."

"OK."

"It's easy."

"Nothing mechanical is easy."

He sighed. "Are you ready?" He watched my face as I slid into the driver's seat, then slammed the door of the truck and walked around to the cab. He got in and sat motionless, waiting.

"I'll need a few instructions, if you don't fucking mind."

"Look, it's hot in Texas. Let's both take it easy."

"I'm trying to."

He looked away to where the road disappeared in mirage past a nothingness, and recited, "Right foot, gas and brake. Left foot, clutch. Now, push in the clutch, put the transmission in neutral, and turn the ignition."

The engine turned over and caught. I wanted to get out of the truck and walk into the brown fields, keep walking. Far off, wheeling birds moved like a pattern of circular dashes in the sky. Something was dead out there, yellowed like the dust and lacy with vanishing. Thurman's voice continued, but closer. He had moved over next to me. "Let the clutch out slowly. Give it gas as you let it out, enough gas at the precise moment, or you'll stall. Now try it, that's right, now the gas. . . ." The truck jerked forward, coughed, jerked, stalled. "Try it again," he said, "a little smoother, gauge the release a little more, there you go—now."

He talked, we jerked and moved, rolled cautiously forward, stopped. The fields remained silent. A mongrel dog ambled out of the brush and sat in the middle of the opposite lane, watching and panting. The dog was maybe twenty pounds of rangy canine, immobile, a desert stone with slit eyes. "Do it again," Thurman murmured. "There you go, give it gas, not too much. OK, OK, we're moving, don't watch the dog, watch the road. Good, good, now—if you go too slow in a gear, you force the engine to lug. Hear that? That's lugging. Give it some gas. . . ."

He kept talking in the close room of the truck, both of us sweating, until the words were meaningless. I repeated the same movements; clutch, gas, shift, brake, downshift, up and down the same mile stretch of road. The mongrel sat watching from one side of the pavement or the other, and the last time we came by, got up and ambled back into the field toward nothing. I pulled jerkily onto the entrance ramp of the freeway as Thurman shifted for me, then onto the highway itself as he applauded.

"Do you forgive me?" I asked.

"For what?" He was watching the road, sitting near enough to grab the wheel. "Check your mirrors. Always know what's coming up on you."

I checked. "For last night," I said. "I'm sorry."

"Don't be sorry. What happened was as likely in this scheme as anything else." He reached under the seat for a pack of cigarettes, still watching the road. "I like you."

"You know something? That one time we slept together in Denver was my first time in six weeks."

"I figured."

"What do you mean?"

"Pay attention—stay in your lane." He turned and glanced behind us. "I mean it seemed like you barely remembered how. There are several like you around. Where are all the girls who were smart and feisty and balled everyone all the time?"

"They got older," I said. "I used to ball anyone too, just based on his eyes or his arms. It's easy when you do it a lot. You get stoned and you don't even think about it. Easy. Like saying hello."

"Guess I missed the boat," he said. "You must have been great to say hello to in the old days. I wish I'd known you then."

"Yeah, I bet you do."

He smiled and lit a cigarette. "But don't you ever miss it? Weren't those days *fun* sometimes? Think about it for a minute. Everyone laughed a lot, didn't they? Group jokes and the old gang. All the dope, everyone with a nickname. Food and big meals and banjos and flutes. People weren't stupid; they just didn't *worry*. The war was over, no one was getting drafted. The girls had birth-control pills and an old man, and once in a while they fucked their best friend's old man, or they all fucked together, and everything was chummy. Right?"

"Sure. That's right."

"Ha," he said.

If I remember right, what we did was this: Rte. 25 from Denver to Albuquerque, 10 to El Paso, 20 to Dallas, 35 to San Antonio, back on 10 to Houston, Beaumont, New Orleans, 65 to Montgomery, 85 to Atlanta and Charlotte, 21 to Wytheville, Virginia, 77 to Charleston and West Virginia; passing through, escaping gravity in a tinny Japanese truck, an imported living quarters. Love in a space capsule, Thurman called it, hate in Houdini's trunk. But there was the windshield and the continual movie past the glass. It was good driving into the movie, good the way the weather changed, the way night and day traded off. Good to camp out for a day or two in a park or a motel, buy a local paper, go to a rummage sale. It was good stopping at the diners and luncheonettes and the daytime bars, or even HoJo's along the interstates: an hour, a few hours, taking off as we'd walked in, as if we had helium in our shoes. Everyone else lived where they stood. They had to live somewhere, and they'd ended up in Tucumcari or Biloxi or Homer, Georgia. All of them, waitresses and bartenders, clerks standing behind motel desks in view of some road, and the signs, place names, streets, houses, were points on a giant connect-the-dots. The truck is what there really was: him and me and the radio, the shell of the space, thin carpet over a floor that reverberated with a hollow *ping* if you stamped down hard. There were the rear-view mirrors turning all that receded sideways, holding the light in glints and angles and the pastels in detached, flat pictures so that any reflected object— car, fence, billboard—seemed just a shape, miraculous in motion. There was the steering wheel, the dash with its square illuminations at night, a few red needles registering numbers. The glove compartment: a flashlight, the truck registration, an aspirin bottle full of white crosses, dope and an aluminum foil envelope of crystal meth in the first-aid box, two caramel bars, a deck of cards. Under the seat were some maps and a few paperbacks, magazines, crumpled wrappers of crackers and health-food cookies and Popsicles, Thurman's harmonica. The radio whined and popped and poured out whatever it caught in the air. In the desert there was nothing but rumbling crackles and shrills; we turned the volume way up till the truck was full of crashing static and rode fast with the roar for miles, all the windows open streaming hot air. But mostly the radio was low. He talked. I talked. We told stories. We argued. We argued a lot as we approached Dallas, where we were going to spend a couple of days with his parents.

"Where did you come from?"
"Thurman, I came from where I'm going."

"I mean in the beginning, like Poland or Scandinavia."

"Wales. But there, in West Virginia, since the 1700s. A land grant. So much land they parceled it out for two hundred years of ten-children families, and only sold the last of it as my father was growing up."

"Sold it to who?"

"The coal companies. Pennsylvania and New York coal companies."

"Uh-huh." He adjusted the rearview mirror. "Why aren't you back there mobilizing against strip mining?"

"Mobilizing? You make it sound like a war." I turned on the radio, and turned it off. "I guess it is a war—New York hippies against New York coal companies." I looked away from him, out the window. "I don't have any excuse, I just wanted to get out."

"You know West Virginia is the only state left where there are no nuclear reactors?" He took a drag on his cigarette and smiled at me across the seat.

"They couldn't put a reactor there," I said. "The land would open like a boil, like an infected Bible, and swallow it." I caught his eye and smiled back. "Impressive. You're up on your eco-lit."

"I'm a good hippie carpenter."

"There are no hippies anymore. There's a fairy tale about working-class visionaries."

"Just a fairy tale? No vision in the working class?"

"Vision everywhere. But in the real working class, vision is half blind. It's romantic to think they really know—"

"You don't think they *know?*" He flicked his cigarette out the window and raised his voice. "They know —they just don't *talk* about it. My grandfather was an Irish Catholic plumber who died of cirrhosis. He used to sit in his chair while the news was on the radio and fold his newspaper into squares. Then he'd unfold it and roll it into a tube, a tight tube the width of a black snake. He'd whack it against the arm of the chair in four-four time, while the announcer kept going and my skinny grandmother grated cabbage in the kitchen by the plates." He checked the mirror and pulled out around a cattle truck. "They knew plenty, sweetheart. You don't know what you're talking about."

"Don't call me sweetheart, and I didn't say they weren't perceptive or frustrated. I said their isolation was real, not an illusion. They stayed in one place and sank with whatever they had. But us—look at us. Roads. Sensation, floating, maps into more of the same. It's a blur, a pattern, a view from an airplane."

"You're a real philosopher, aren't you? What do you want? You want to sink, righteous and returned to your roots? Is that it?"

"I can't."

"Can't what?"

"Sink. I don't know how."

"Oh, Christ. Will you shut up and light that joint before we pull into Dallas?"

I took the joint out of his cigarette pack and looked for matches.

"Here," he said, and threw them at me. "No wonder you live alone and sleep on floors. You're ponderous and depressed. Nothing is any worse than it's ever been."

"No," I said, "only more detached."

"Detachment is an ageless virtue. Try a little Zen."

"I am," I said, and lit the joint. "I'm living in Zen, highway Zen, the wave of the future."

He didn't laugh. We pulled into Dallas and Thurman finished the joint at a roadside park in sight of three Taco Bells, a McDonald's, and a Sleepytime Motel. He squinted behind the smoke, drawing in. "What does your dad do?" he asked.

"Retired."

"OK. What *did* he do?"

"Roads. He built roads."

"Highways?"

"No. Two-lane roads, in West Virginia. Hairpin turns."

The joint glowed in his fingers. Dusk had fallen, a gray shade. The air was heavy and hot, full of random horns and exhaust. I could see the grit on Thurman's skin and feel the same sweaty pallor on my face.

"What is your father like?" I asked him.

He exhaled, his eyes distanced. "My father is seventy-one. Lately he's gone a little flaky."

We sat in silence until the dope was gone. Thurman turned on the ignition. "You'll have your own bedroom at my parents' house," he said, "and I sure hope your sheets aren't too heavy."

The house was a big old-fashioned saltbox on an acre of lawn, incongruous among the split-levels, badly in need of paint. Drainpipes hung at angles from the roof and the grass was cut in strange swaths, grown tall as field weeds in patches. An old Chevy station wagon sat on blocks in front of the garage. Thurman and I sat in the driveway, in the cab of the Datsun, looking.

"They've gotten worse, or he has. I've hired kids to cut the grass for him and he won't let them on the property."

"Did they know we were coming?"

"Yes."

The front door opened and Thurman's mother appeared. She was small and thin, her arms folded across her chest, and it was obvious from the way she peered into middle distance that she couldn't really see us.

"You go first," I said, "she'll want to see you alone."

He got out of the truck and approached her almost

carefully, then lifted her off the ground in an embrace. She didn't seem big enough to ever have been his mother, but a few minutes later, as she looked searchingly into my face, her handshake was surprisingly firm.

The inside rooms smelled of faded potpourri and trapped air despite the air-conditioner. Only the smallest downstairs rooms seemed lived in: the kitchen, a breakfast nook, a small den with a television and fold-out couch made up as a bed. The large living room was empty except for a rocking chair in the middle of the naked floor. The room had been dismantled and holes in the plaster repaired; three large portraits in frames of uniform size were covered with painter's cloths and propped against the wall. Above them were the faded squares of space where they'd hung.

"Oh," I said, "you're painting."

"Well." She surveyed the room. "We were going to paint three years ago, but we never did." She smiled.

Upstairs the hall was dusty. Plaster had fallen off the walls in chunks and exposed the wooden wallboards. Bits of newspaper and chips of paint littered the floor; the master bedroom was clean but unused, and the other bedrooms seemed deserted: furniture pushed to the center of the floor, beds filmed with a fine dust.

"You take this room," Thurman said, "I'll be across the hall." He picked up a broom and began sweeping off the mattress. "I'll get you some sheets."

I said nothing.

He put the broom down. "Look, it was me who got the living room ready for painting—two years ago, not three. I'd hired painters to do that room and the outside; my father called them and told them not to come." Thurman stepped over to the window, looking down at the lawn through streaked glass. "But that grass. . . . Still, he's known I was coming for six weeks, maybe he planned this whole scenario. He won't let

me buy him a power mower or do any chores for him.
We fight about it every time I come home. This time
I'm not fighting."

"Why is he mad at you?"

"Because I bailed out eleven years ago. Eleven years
is a lot of mad." Thurman looked up at me. "And
don't be surprised if he doesn't talk to you. His hearing isn't really so bad but he pretends to be deaf. He'll
act busy the whole time we're here."

We sat at the edge of the concrete patio in deck
chairs.

"My father was famous. He was known as the best
high school football coach in the history of the state
of Texas. Universities offered him jobs, but he
wouldn't move his family, he wouldn't leave this
house." Thurman shook the ice in his empty glass and
looked levelly toward the old wooden garage. His father stood in the open doorway with the push mower,
frowned down at the turning blades as he pushed the
contraption into the grass of the side lawn. "I knew he
was famous from the time I was a kid. And my brothers
were famous, six and eight years older than me, both
of them drafted to play ball at SMU after starring on
his teams. And later I was famous, but not as famous
as them. I played on my father's last team and we went
to the play-offs; he was sixty years old."

The mower made its high scissoring whirr as the old
man shoved it back and forth. The slender wooden
handle was as gray and weathered as barn board.

"His kids aren't going to cart him off anywhere, and
no one in this posh neighborhood had better try it
either," Thurman said. "He was here first. And there
are still people around who remember my father. If he
wants to let his house fall down, or set it on fire or blow
it up, I guess he's entitled."

I watched Thurman's father. He'd barely acknowledged my presence, though he'd discussed the mower with Thurman as they both knelt to wipe the blades clean with a rag. The old man was lean and stooped but he didn't seem fragile.

Thurman picked up the pint bottle between our chairs and colored the ice in his glass with bourbon.

"Did you win?" I asked him.

"What?"

"Win the championships, the last ones."

"By the skin of our teeth. We were behind and tried a long last-resort run as the clock ran out. I played end and blocked for our quarterback, a fast little Mexican named Martinez. I was the last one with him, thought it was over and took two of their backs as Martinez jumped the pile of us. I wanted to knock myself out, too much of a coward to stay conscious if we lost. I came to ten minutes later with a concussion, and we'd won."

"Was your father standing over you?"

"No, he was up there accepting the trophy. Then he came and balanced it on my chest as they lifted me onto the stretcher—big gold monstrosity with three pedestals that multiplied and looked like infinity. I wasn't seeing too clearly. That was 1964; things were just beginning to focus." He looked over at me. "You were about twelve years old then."

I looked back at him. "You didn't go to SMU."

"Not a chance. Football nearly killed me. I couldn't read print for two weeks." He sank lower in the deck chair, stroking the lush grass with his foot. His legs were long and muscular and fair. "If I'd hit an inch more to the right, I'd have bought myself a box. But even without the concussion, I was sick of it. I went to Colorado and ski-bummed and ran dope up from Mexico and went to school, did the Peace Corps trip. Didn't see my father for years."

"Why didn't the war get you? The concussion?"

"No. Knees. Got my brother though, the middle one. Killed him. He didn't even have to go. He was almost twenty-eight years old and enlisted, like a fool. My father thought it was the right thing to do. They shipped him over there and killed him in nine weeks. Nineteen sixty-eight. Saw my father at the funeral. Kept saying to me, 'Barnes was on drugs, wasn't he. They're all on drugs over there. He wouldn't have died otherwise, he was an athlete. Still worked out every day. Drugs killed him.' I said, 'Dad, the war killed him. War doesn't give a shit about athletes.' I did two tours in the Peace Corps after that. I just wanted to stay the fuck out of the country."

"Thurman . . . Thurman?" His mother's voice wavered out across the lawn. I turned and saw her at the kitchen window. "Supper," she called, "come on in now. . . ." Her every phrase was punctuated with a silence.

Thurman didn't move.

"Do you come back here often?" I asked. "How much do you see them?"

"Once a year, maybe twice. He's getting old. There's not much more time to figure it out, any of it."

I couldn't sleep. I crept down the stairs to get a glass of water. Disoriented, I turned the wrong corner into the dim living room and found myself facing the shrouded portraits. I knelt beside the last. If I looked now, no one would know; carefully, silently, I pulled the cloth away. First, a shine of glass, then, in moonlight, the features of a face. I thought it was Barnes, the dead brother, serious and young in his black suit, already marked—but no, the eyes—it was Thurman. I stared, puzzled.

"High school graduation," he said behind me. "We were all eighteen." The rocking chair creaked. "What are you doing up?"

"I couldn't sleep."

"No one sleeps much in this house."

"Who else is awake?"

"My mother. I heard her in the kitchen. When I came downstairs, she went back to bed. That's the way we do it around here." He nodded at the closed door of the little den. "She seems to have had a few drinks."

"Is that usual?"

"Who's to say? Her drinking progresses, like everything." He took a drag off his cigarette, and the glow of the ash lit his face for an instant. "She forgets things when she drinks. Conveniently."

"I doubt it's just convenience."

"What else would it be?"

I shrugged. "Pain?"

Thurman sighed. "You never know when to keep your mouth shut. Do you think I want to sit here in this house at three in the morning and talk about pain?"

"No." I could see him very clearly in the darkness. I moved closer and touched his forehead. "You talk, Thurman, and let me know when I should speak. I'll say whatever you want."

He stood, and put his arms around my shoulders and held me. We turned to go upstairs, then Thurman paused. We heard broken words, a murmuring. He stepped closer to the den and stood listening, then pushed the door softly open. His mother stood near us in her bathrobe, an empty glass in her hand. She seemed unaware of us and looked up slowly. The dim little room was crowded with furniture and smelled faintly of bourbon. Thurman's sleeping father was in shadow.

"Mom, you should be in bed. You might fall." He walked over to her and took the glass. "I'll put this in the kitchen for you."

She stopped Thurman and grabbed his wrist. "Listen," she said slowly, in a tone of confidence, "Barnes never answers a letter, never calls. Where is he?"

Thurman led her to the bed. "Don't pull that on me."

"She isn't," I whispered, "she really—"

Now she was sitting on the edge of the mattress. Thurman put his hands on her shoulders and shook her once, gently. She looked him in the eye. "Who is that girl?" she said.

"A friend of mine, Mom, you met her earlier today. Here, lie down before you wake Dad."

She said nothing and clutched Thurman's hand; he leaned closer involuntarily. Her eyes widened, her face caught in the light of the one lamp. For a moment I could see how he favored her, how she must have looked at twenty-five: the clear, ruddy complexion, the cast and blue directness of the eyes, the thick auburn hair, maybe worn in a braid to her waist. This close, their faces nearly touched. Her profile was a broken, feminine version of his. I turned away.

"Mom, lie down."

"Don't you be leaving again now."

"Go to sleep, get some rest."

"I don't sleep. Don't you be leaving."

"Thurman," I said. I heard him straighten. Her body shifted in the bed, then he was beside me in the hallway, pulling their door shut. He stood breathing quietly, listening. No sound. The mottled living-room walls lightened as our eyes took in the dark again. Colors of dun and gray, cracked. In one corner, patches of missing plaster were ragged star shapes where the boards showed through. I reached for him.

"I shouldn't come here," he said.

"It's all right."

He stood there, looking at their closed door. "Who saves who?" he said.

I pulled his head down, close to me, touching him, his face. "Let's sleep outside."

I got some blankets and we spread them in the yard. The acacia bushes were a thick bank, bulbous and shadowy, smelling of sweet dust.

Then we hit New Orleans. Checked into a motel. Went to that bar where everyone was dancing.

What happened was scary and stupid, and whirling and sick and drunkenly predictable, and in the cards from the first. Afterward, things were different, and Thurman had no illusions about saving me. He must have worked things out himself after he left the bar alone, while he was waiting for me all night in that motel, the aqua drapes moving over the air vents behind the blue glow of the television. I remember almost all the motel rooms, and I remember that one especially, the big Zenith console TV and those cheap drapes blue as fired gas. In seven hours, Thurman could have watched three movies and twelve sets of commercials. He left me at the bar at two A.M. and I pulled into the motel parking lot in a taxi at nine. He was just drawing tight the ropes of the tarp and the door to the room was standing open. I got in the truck after exchanging one look with him, and nothing else passed between us until Georgia, when we got in the lake.

Then, we kept going.

"Don't drive in the fast lane unless you're passing." Thurman, his voice gravelly with wakefulness.

"Why not? I pass everything anyway, so I might as well stay in the fast lane. I like fast lanes."

"Oh, you do. Well. Someone even faster is going to come roaring up and eat your ass. How will you like that?" He switched off the radio. "God dammit, will you listen to me for a minute?"

I looked at him once, and kept driving.

"Pull the truck off the road," he said.

"Are you going to beat me, Thurman?"

"Pull off, right now."

I pulled off on the berm and shifted into neutral. A cattle truck passed us doing eighty, rocking the cab. There was a bawl and a smell and it was gone. Thurman sat with his back to the passenger door. "Take your hands off the wheel," he said.

"Thurman, what is this?"

"I'll tell you what it is. You're in trouble, and no fast lane is going to help."

"I don't want help. I'll just keep going until I find a way to get off."

"Good for you, sweetheart."

"Screw you."

"Hey, don't worry. You'll get no help from me. Last time I quit fast lanes I made myself a promise—no more Samaritan crap."

"You're all heart."

"You'd better worry about your own heart. You're the one with the racing pulse and the shakes, sleeping on floors and getting picked up by three jokers in a disco."

"OK, Thurman."

"Not OK. I've been there, I know what you're doing. You spend half your time in a full-throttle heat and the other half holding on when you realize how fast you're going. You don't even come up for air. Your insides are blue because you're suffocating. Your guts shake because you scare yourself. You get close enough to see death doesn't give a shit about you."

I turned off the ignition and the truck was silent. Noises of the highway went by, loud vibrations that took on the quality of musical tones. I don't know how long we sat there, maybe only a few minutes.

"Death isn't supposed to give a shit," I said, "is it?

Death is a zero. Blue like ice is blue. Perfect. Barnes is perfect. Your father will be perfect, my father. All of us, cold and perfect." Thurman moved close to me across the seat. We were both sweating. He pulled his damp T-shirt away from his body and touched the cloth to my face. I whispered, as if someone were listening to us, "I don't mind the heat. I guess I want the heat."

"I know, I know. And we got heat. We got plenty of heat for you here in the USA."

The cotton of his shirt was soft and worn. "Let's drive," I said. "Who's driving?"

"What the hell. You drive."

"Do you want me to stay in the slow lane?"

"I don't care. Drive on the berm, drive up the median, drive upside down."

I pulled onto the highway with a few jerks but no grinding of gears. Thurman turned the radio back on to a gospel broadcast. There was a choir singing strong and heavy about a land on high in the sunshine; their group vibrato wavered in the dashboard.

"You're something else," came Thurman's voice. "You never did take your fucking hands off the wheel."

"I guess I didn't."

"Jesus. I don't know why I should worry about you. You'll probably come out of this with a new refrigerator and a trip to Mexico."

"Sure I will. A trip to the Gringo Hotel in Juárez, where they eat dog and hand out diseases."

He lit a cigarette and gazed out the window.

Close home, we drove through Virginia mountains in the rain. I had moments of total panic in which I seemed to be falling, spread-eagled, far away from myself, my whole body growing rapidly smaller and smaller. I could feel the spinning, the sensation of dropping. I held tightly to the door handle and concentrated on the moving windshield wiper in front of me, carefully watching its metal rib and rubber blade. I willed myself into the sound, the swish of movement and water, dull *thwack* as the blade landed on either side of its half-rotation. Runnels of rain and the tracks of their descent took me in; I could smell rain through the glass, smell clean water and washed leaves. I sat very still and the spinning of my own body slowed; the aperture of my senses widened, opened in a clear focus. Then I could feel the seat under my hips again and my feet on the floor of the truck, the purr, the vibration of engine. The capsule of the truck's cab existed around me: damp leather, a faint musk of bodies. Close to me, Thurman would be humming tunelessly to himself, staring ahead into the rainy mountains and the twisting road.

The last night, we camped out in a National Forest. Nearly dusk already, and the ground was damp; I raked leaves into a broad pile to make us a softer bed, provide some insulation. The mountains and the air smelled of autumn, soil, rich mulch.

"Sit down here and get warm." Thurman piled more wood on the fire. "Enjoy the wide open spaces. Tomorrow you're safe, if not sound. Remember safe? You'll get used to it again real fast." He blew into the fire, then leaned back and gazed at me through a wavering column of heat. "You scared?"

I touched the border of stones we'd built to surround the campfire. The stones were rough, and warming. "The shakes are coming, right now," I told him. "I can feel them."

"No," he said, "you're OK. I'm sitting right here looking at you."

"You can't always see them. Sometimes they're just in my gut."

He took one of my hands and squeezed it, then kneaded my palm and worked down each finger. He pulled hard on each joint and talked as though neither of us were paying any attention to how hard he was pulling. "You're fine," he said. "We're going to lay down in the leaves and take some deep breaths, then all those jangles will go somewhere else."

I closed my eyes and I could feel the shade creeping across the leaves. Leaves fell slowly at long intervals, dropping with a papery sound. "I think it's better if I sit here and cry," I said.

"You can't. You're not a crier."

"Let me try. Tell me a bad story."

"I got no bad stories." He picked me up in his arms and knelt to put me on the ground. The leaves were thick under us, old leaves smelling of dry mud. "Only one story," Thurman said. "We've been in that truck three weeks. A few more hours, and you're home." I remembered a song that used to play on AM radio when I was gawky and twelve, the tallest girl in the class. *Be my little baby, Won't you be my darling, be my baby now. . . .* I laughed. That's what I was, a baby, a frozen six-year-old baby going back to the start of the cold.

"Funny story, huh?" He kissed my eyes. "Don't get hysterical. I won't force you. Male pride, the Code—"

"You couldn't rape anyone. You might get mad enough to start, but at the crucial moment your equipment would fail you."

"You're right. I was born with a kindly cock." I felt his legs against me, his hard stomach, the buckle of his belt. He unfastened it to keep the metal from hurting me and touched me low on my hips.

"You get turned on when you're paternal," I said. "You're going to be hell on your daughter."

"You're hell on me," he said. "You'll be someone's good lover someday when I'm drinking beer alone in a tavern and hearing the pinball machines."

I opened his shirt and pants and slid down against him. Lake smell, like Georgia, taste of a bruise. He was in my mouth, his hands in my hair, then he moved to stop me and turned my face up. He bent over me, holding my arms, his eyes angry and surprised and wet. "No," he said.

"Thurman." I was crying. "I just want you to drop me off tomorrow. Me and the suitcases and the box of books. I don't want to see you meet my mother, none of that. All right? Please."

The cold was moving up through the ground. He felt me shiver in the dark and pulled me on top of him. I lay there and he held me with one arm. His chest was wider than my shoulders, smelling of the cold tinge of the leaves. He was awake, smoking a cigarette and staring into the trees. He exhaled with a long breath.

"It's all timing," he said. "This whole joke. Timing and the shakes."

"You're better off without me. You don't want any fast lanes."

He moved his warm heavy hand to the back of my head. "I'll tell you this about fast lanes. Don't close your eyes. Keep watching every minute. Watch in your sleep. If you're careful you can make it: the fast shift, the one right move. Sooner or later you'll see your chance."

BLUEGILL

*H*ello my little bluegill, little shark face. Fanged one, sucker, hermaphrodite. Rose, bloom in the fog of the body; see how the gulls arch over us, singing their raucous squalls. They bring you sweetmeats, tiny mice, spiders with clasped legs. In their old claws, claws of eons, reptilian sleep, they cradle shiny rocks and bits of glass. Boat in my blood, I dream you furred and sharp-toothed, loping in snow mist on a tundra far from the sea. I believe you are male; will I make you husband, uncle, brother? Feed you in dark movie houses of a city we haven't found? This village borders waves, roofs askew, boards vacant. I'll leave here with two suitcases and a music box, but what of you, little boot, little head with two eyes? I talk to you, bone of my coming, bone of an earnest receipt. I feel you now, steaming in the cave of the womb.

Here there are small fires. I bank a blaze in the iron stove and waken ringed in damp; how white air seeps inside the cracked houses, in the rattled doors and sills. We have arrived and settled in a house that groans, shifting its mildewed walls. The rains have come, rolling mud yards of fishermen's shacks down a dirt road to the curling surf. Crabs' claws bleach in spindled grass; dogs tear the discarded shells and drag them in rain. They fade from orange to peach to the pearl of the disembodied. Smells crouch and pull, moving in wet air. Each night crates of live crab are delivered to the smokehouse next door. They clack and crawl, a lumbering mass whose mute antennae click a filament of loss. Ocean is a ream of white meat, circles in a muscular brain. I eat these creatures; their flesh is sweet and flaky. They are voiceless, fluid in their watery dusk, trapped in nets a mile from the rocky cliffs. You are some kin to them, floating in your own dark sac.

Kelp floats a jungle by the pier, armless, legless, waving long sea hair, tresses submerged and rooty. These plants are bulbs and a nipple, rounded snouts weaving their tubular tails. Little boys find them washed up on the beach, wet, rubbery, smelling of salt. They hold the globular heads between their legs and ride them like stick horses. They gallop off, long tails dragging tapered in the sand. They run along the water in groups of three or four, young centaurs with no six-guns whose tracks evoke visions of mythical reptiles. They run all the way to the point, grow bored, fight, scatter; finally one comes back alone, preoccupied, dejected, dragging the desultory tail in one hand as the foamy surf tugs it seaward. I watch him; I pretend you see him too, see it all with your X-ray vision, your soft eyes, their honeycomb facets judging the souls of all failed boys. We watch the old ones, the young ones, the boats bobbing their rummy cargoes of traps and nets and hooks.

I sit at the corner table of the one restaurant, diner near the water where fishermen drink coffee at six A.M. I arrive later, when the place is nearly empty, when the sun slants on toward noon and the coffee has aged to a pungent syrup. The waitress is the postmaster's wife; she knows I get one envelope a month, that I cash one check at MacKinsie's Market, that I rent a postbox on a six-month basis. She spots my ringless hands, the gauntness in my face, the calcium pills I pull out of my purse in a green medicinal bottle. She recognizes my aversion to eggs; she knows that blur in my pupils, blur and flare, wavering as though I'm sucked inward by a small interior flame. You breathe, adhered to a cord. Translucent astronaut, your eyes change days like a calendar watch. The fog surrounds us, drifting between craggy hills like an insubstantial blimp, whale shape that breaks up and spreads. Rock islands rise from the olive sea; they've caught seed in the wind and sit impassive, totems bristling with pine. Before long they will split and speak, revealing a long-trapped Hamlin piper and a troop of children whose bodies are musical and perfect, whose thoughts have grown pure. The children translate each wash of light on the faces of their stone capsules; they feel each nuance of sun and hear the fog as a continuous sigh, drifted breath of the one giant to whom they address their prayers. They have grown no taller and experienced no disease; they sleep in shifts. The piper has made no sound since their arrival. His inert form has become luminous and faintly furred. He is a father fit for animalistic angels whose complex mathematical games evolve with the centuries, whose hands have become transparent from constant handling of quartz pebbles and clear agates. They have no interest in talk or travel; they have developed beyond the inhabitants of countries and communicate only with the unborn. They repudiate the music that tempted them and create it now within themselves, a silent version expressed in numerals, angles, complicated slitherings. They are mobile as lizards and opaque as those small blind fish found in the still waters of caves. Immortal, they become their own children. Their memories of a long-ago journey are layered as genetics: how the sky eclipsed, how the piped melody was transformed as they walked into the sea and were submerged. The girls and smaller boys remember their dresses blousing, swirling like anemones. The music entered a new dimension, felt inside them like cool fingers, formal as a harpsichord yet buoyant, wild; they were taken up with it days at a time. . . .

Here in the diner, there is a jukebox that turns up loud. High school kids move the tables back and dance on Friday nights. They are sixteen, tough little girls who disdain makeup and smoke Turkish cigarettes, or last year's senior boys who can't leave the village. Already they're hauling net on their fathers' boats, learning a language of profanity and back-slapping, beer, odd tumescent dawns as the other boats float out of sight. They want to marry at twenty, save money, acquire protection from the weather. But the girls are like colts, skittish and lean; they've read magazines, gone to rock concerts, experimented with drugs and each other. They play truant and drive around all day in VWs, listen to AM radio in the rain and swish of the wipers, dream of graduation and San Francisco, L.A., Mexico. They go barefoot in the dead of winter and seldom eat; their faces are pale and dewy from the moist air, the continuous rains. They show up sullen-eyed for the dances and get younger as the evening progresses, drinking grocery-store mixed drinks from thermoses in boys' cars. Now they are willing to dance close and imitate their mothers. Music beats in the floor like a heart; movie-theme certainty and the simple lyric of hold-me-tight. I pause on my nightly walks and watch their silhouettes on the windows; nearby the dock pylons stand up mossy and beaten, slap of the water intimate and old. Boys sit exchanging hopeful stories, smoking dope. Sometimes they whistle. They can't see my shape in my bulky coat. Once, one of them followed me home and waited beyond the concrete porch and the woodpile; I saw his face past the thrown ellipses of light. I imagined him in my bed, smooth-skinned and physically happy, no knowledge but intent. He would address you through my skin, nothing but question marks. Instructed to move slowly from behind, he would be careful, tentative, but forget at the end and push hard. There is no danger; you are floating, interior and protected; but it's that rhythmic lapsing of my love for you that would frighten; we have been alone so long. So I am true to you; I shut off the light and he goes away. In some manner, I am in your employ; I feed my body to feed you and buy my food with money sent me because of you. I am very nearly married to you; and it is only here, a northwestern fishing village in the rains, constant rain, that the money comes according to bargain, to an understanding conceived in your interest. I have followed you though you cannot speak, only fold, unfold. Blueprint, bone and toenail, sapphire. You must know it all from the beginning, never suffer the ignorance of boys with vestigial tails and imagined guns. I send you all these secrets in my blood; they wash through you like dialysis. You are the animal and the saint, snow-blind, begun in blindness . . . you must break free of me like a weasel or a fox, fatherless, dark as the seals that bark like haunted men from the rocks, far away, their calls magnified in the distance, in the twilight.

Ghost, my solitaire, I'll say your father was a horse, a Percheron whose rippled mane fell across my shoulders, whose tight hide glimmered, who shivered and made small winged insects rise into the air. A creature large-eyed, velvet. Long bone of the face broad as a forearm, back broad as sleep. Massive. Looking from the side of the face, a peripheral vision innocent, instinctual.

But no, there were many fathers. There was a truck, a rattling of nuts and bolts, a juggling of emergencies. Suede carpenter's apron spotted with motor oil, clothes kept in stacked crates. There were hands never quite clean and later, manicured hands. A long car with mechanical windows that *zimmed* as they moved smoothly up and down, impenetrable as those clear shells separating the self from a dreamed desire (do you dream? of long foldings, channels, imageless dreams of fish, long turnings, echoed sounds and shading waters). In between, there were faces in many cars, road maps and laced boots, hand-printed signs held by the highway exits, threats from ex-cons, cajoling salesmen, circling patrolmen. There were counters, tables, eight-hour shifts, grease-stained menus, prices marked over three times, regulars pathetic and laughing, cheap regulation nylons, shoes with ridged soles, creamers filled early as a truck arrives with sugared doughnuts smelling of vats and heat. Men cursed in heavy accents, living in motor hum of the big dishwashers, overflowed garbage pails, ouzo at the end of the day. Then there were men across hallways, stair rails, men with offices, married men and their secretaries, empty bud vase on a desk. Men in elevators, white shirts ironed by a special Chinaman on Bleecker. Sanitary weekend joggers, movie reviewers, twenty-seventh floor, manufactured air, salon haircuts, long lunches, table-cloths and wine. Rooftop view, jets to cut swelling white slashes in the sky. And down below, below rooftops and clean charmed rhymes, the dark alleys meandered; those same alleys that crisscross a confusion of small towns. Same sideways routes and wishful arrivals, eye-level gravel, sooty perfumes, pale grass seeding in the stones. Bronzed light in casts of season: steely and blue, smoke taste of winters; the pinkish dark of any thaw; then coral falling in greens, summer mix of rot and flowers; autumn a burnt red, orange darkened to rust and scab. All of it men and faces, progression, hands come to this and you, grown inside me like one reminder.

He faced me over a café table, showed me the town on a map. No special reason, he said, he'd been here once; a quiet place, pretty, it would do. One geography was all he asked in the arrangement, the "interruption." He mentioned his obligation and its limits; he mentioned our separate paths. I don't ask here if they know him, I don't speculate. I've left him purely, as though you came to me after a voyage of years, as though you flew like a seed, saw them all and won me from them. I've lived with you all these months, grown cowish and full of you, yet I don't name you except by touch, curl, gesture. Wake and sleep, slim minnow, luminous frog. There are clues and riddles, pages in the book of the body, stones turned and turned. Each music lasts, forgetful, surfacing in the aisles of anonymous shops.

Music, addition and subtraction, Pavlovian reminder of scenes becoming, only dreamed. Evenings I listen to the radio and read fairy tales; those first lies, those promises. Directions are clear: crumbs in the woods, wolves in red hoods, the prince of temptation more believable as an enchanted toad. He is articulate and patient; there is the music of those years in the deep well, *plunk* of moisture, *whish* of the wayward rain, and finally the face of rescue peering over the stone rim like a moon. Omens burst into bloom; each life evolved to a single moment: the ugly natural, shrunken and wise, cradled in a palm fair as camellias.

Knot of cells, where is your voice? Here there are no books of instructions. There is the planed edge of the oaken table, the blond rivulets of the wood. There is a lamp in a dirty shade and the crouched stove hunkering its blackness around a fiery warmth. All night I sit, feeling the glow from a couch pulled close to the heat. Stirring the ashes, feeding, feeding, eating the fire with my skin. The foghorn cries through the mist in the bay: *bawaah, bawaah,* weeping of an idiot sheep, steady, measured as love. At dawn I'm standing by the window and the fishing boats bob like toys across the water, swaying their toothpick masts. Perfect mirage, they glisten and fade. Morning is two hours of sun as the season turns, a dime gone silver and thin. The gnarled plants are wild in their pots, spindly and bent. Gnats sleep on the leaves, inaugurating flight from a pearly slime on the windowpane. Their waftings are broken and dreamy, looping in the cold air of the house slowly, so slowly that I clap my hands and end them. Staccato, flash: that quick chord of once-upon-a-time.

Faraway I was a child, resolute, small, these same eyes in my head sinking back by night. Always I waited for you, marauder, collector, invisible pea in the body. I called you stones hidden in corners, paper fish with secret meanings, clothespin doll. Alone in my high bed, the dark, the dark; I shook my head faster, faster, rope of long hair flying across my shoulders like a switch, a scented tail. Under the bed, beyond the frothy curtain duster, I kept a menagerie of treasures and dust: discarded metallic jewelry, glass rhinestones pried from their settings, old gabardine suitcoat from a box in the basement, lipsticks, compacts with cloudy mirrors, slippers with pompoms, a man's blue silk tie embossed with tiny golf clubs. At night I crawled under wrapped in my sheets, breathing the buried smell, rattling the bed slats with my knees. I held my breath till the whole floor moved, plethora of red slashes; saw you in guises of lightning and the captive atmosphere.

Now a storm rolls the house in its paws. Again, men are lost and a hull washes up on the rocks. All day search copters hover and sweep. Dipping low, they chop the air for survivors and flee at dusk. The bay lies capped and draggled, rolling like water sloshed in a bowl. Toward nightfall, wind taps like briers on the windowpanes. We go out, down to the rocks and the shore. The forgotten hull lies breaking and splintered, only a slab of wood. The bay moves near it like a sleeper under sheets, murmuring, calling more rain. Animal in me, fish in a swim, I tell you *everything drowns.* I say *believe me if you are mine,* but you push like a fist with limbs. I feel your eyes searching, your gaze trapped in the dark like a beam of light. Then your vision transcends my skin: finally, I see them too, the lost fishermen, their faces framed in swirling hair like the heads of women. They are pale and blue, glowing, breathing with a pulse in their throats. They rise streaming tattered shirts, shining like mother-of-pearl. They rise moving toward us, round-mouthed, answering, answering the spheres of your talk. I am only witness to a language. The air is yours; it is water circling in like departure.

SOMETHING THAT HAPPENED

I am in the base-
ment sorting clothes, whites with whites, colors with
colors, delicates with delicates—it's a segregated
world—when my youngest child yells down the steps.
She yells when I'm in the basement, always, angrily, as
if I've slipped below the surface and though she's
twenty-one years old she can't believe it.

"Do you know what day it is? I mean do you *know*
what day it is, Kay?" It's this new thing of calling me
by my first name. She stands groggy-eyed, surveying
her mother.

I say, "No, Angela, so what does that make me?"

Now my daughter shifts into second, narrows those baby blues I once surveyed in such wonder and prayed *Lord, lord, this is the last.*

"Well, never mind," she says. "I've made you breakfast." And she has, eggs and toast and juice and flowers on the porch. Then she sits and watches me eat it, twirling her fine gold hair.

Halfway through the eggs it dawns on me, my ex– wedding anniversary. Angela, under the eyeliner and blue jeans you're a haunted and ancient presence. When most children can't remember an anniversary, Angela can't forget it. Every year for five years, she has pushed me to the brink of remembrance.

"The trouble with you," she finally says, "is that you don't care enough about yourself to remember what's been important in your life."

"Angela," I say, "in the first place I haven't been married for five years, so I no longer have a wedding anniversary to remember."

"That doesn't matter" (twirling her hair, not scowling). "It's still something that happened."

Two years ago I had part of an ulcerated stomach removed and I said to the kids, "Look, I can't worry for you anymore. If you get into trouble, don't call me. If you want someone to take care of you, take care of each other." So the three older girls packed Angela off to college and her brother drove her there. Since then I've gradually resumed my duties. Except that I was inconspicuously absent from my daughters' weddings. I say inconspicuously because, thank God, all of them were hippies who got married in fields without benefit of aunts and uncles. Or mothers. But Angela reads *Glamour,* and she'll ask me to her wedding. Though Mr. Charm has yet to appear in any permanent guise, she's already gearing up for it. Pleadings. Remonstrations. Perhaps a few tears near the end. But I shall hold firm, I hate sacrificial offerings of my own flesh. "I can't help it," I'll joke, "I have a weak stomach, only half of it is there."

Angela sighs, perhaps foreseeing it all. The phone is ringing. And slowly, there she goes. By the time she picks it up, cradles the receiver to her brown neck, her voice is normal. Penny-bright, and she spends it fast. I look out the screened porch on the alley and the clean garbage cans. It seems to me that I remembered everything before the kids were born. I say kids as though they appeared collectively in a giant egg, my stomach. When actually there were two years, then one year, then two, then three between them. The Child-Bearing Years, as though you stand there like a blossomed pear tree and the fruit plops off. Eaten or rotted to seed to start the whole thing all over again.

Angela has fixed too much food for me. She often does. I don't digest large amounts so I eat small portions six times a day. The dog drags his basset ears to my feet, waits for the plate. And I give it to him, urging him on so he'll gobble it fast and silent before Angela comes back.

Dear children, I always confused my stomach with my womb. Lulled into confusion by nearly four pregnant years I heard them say, "Oh, you're eating for two," as if the two organs were directly connected by a small tube. In the hospital I was convinced they had removed my uterus along with half of my stomach. The doctors, at an end of patience, labeled my decision an anxiety reaction. And I reacted anxiously by demanding an X ray so I could see that my womb was still there.

Angela returns, looks at the plate, which I have forgotten to pick up, looks at the dog, puts her hand on my shoulder.

"I'm sorry," she says.

"Well," I say.

Angela twists her long fingers, her fine thin fingers with their smooth knuckles, twists the diamond ring her father gave her when she was sixteen.

"Richard," I'd said to my husband, "she's your daughter, not your fiancée."

"Kay," intoned the husband, the insurance agent, the successful adjuster of claims, "she's only sixteen once. This ring is a gift, our love for Angela. She's beautiful, she's blossoming."

"Richard," I said, shuffling Maalox bottles and planning my bland lunch, "diamonds are not for blossoms. They're for those who need a piece of the rock." At which Richard laughed heartily, always amused at my cynicism regarding the business that principally buttered my bread. Buttered his bread, because by then I couldn't eat butter.

"What is it you're afraid to face?" asked Richard. "What is it in your life you can't control? You're eating yourself alive. You're dissolving your own stomach."

"Richard," I said, "it's a tired old story. I have this husband who wants to marry his daughter."

"I want you to see a psychiatrist," said Richard, tightening his expertly knotted tie. "That's what you need, Kay, a chance to talk it over with someone who's objective."

"I'm not interested in objectives," I said. "I'm interested in shrimp and butter sauce, Tabasco, hot chilis, and an end of pain."

"Pain never ends," said Richard.

"Oh, Richard," I said, "no wonder you're the King of the Southeast Division."

"Look," he said, "I'm trying to put four kids through college and one wife through graduate school. I'm starting five investment plans now so when our kids get married no one has to wait twenty-five years to finish a dissertation on George Eliot like you did. Really, am I such a bad guy? I don't remember forcing you into any of this. And your goddamn stomach has to quit digesting itself. I want you to see a psychiatrist."

"Richard," I said, "if our daughters have five children in eight years—which most of them won't, being members of Zero Population Growth who quote *Diet for a Small Planet* every Thanksgiving—they may still be slow with Ph.D.s despite your investment plans."

Richard untied his tie and tied it again. "Listen," he said. "Plenty of women with five children have Ph.Ds."

"Really," I said. "I'd like to see those statistics."

"I suppose you resent your children's births," he said, straightening his collar. "Well, just remember, the last one was your miscalculation."

"And the first one was yours," I said.

It's true. We got pregnant, as Richard affectionately referred to it, in a borrowed bunk bed on Fire Island. It was the eighth time we'd slept together. Richard gasped that of course he'd take care of things, had he ever failed me? But I had my first orgasm and no one remembered anything.

After the fourth pregnancy and first son, Richard was satisfied. Angela, you were born in a bad year. You were expensive, your father was starting in insurance after five years as a high school principal. He wanted the rock, all of it. I had a rock in my belly we thought three times was dead. So he swore his love to you, with that ring he thee guiltily wed. Sweet Sixteen, does she remember? She never forgets.

Angela pasted sugar cubes to pink ribbons for a week, Sweet Sixteen party favors she read about in *Seventeen,* while the older girls shook their sad heads. Home from colleges in Ann Arbor, Boston, Berkeley, they stared aghast at their golden-haired baby sister, her Villager suits, the ladybug stickpin in her blouses. Angela owned no blue jeans; her boyfriend opened the car door for her and carried her books home. They weren't heavy, he was a halfback. Older sister no. 3: "Don't you have arms?" Older sister no. 2: "He'll take it out of your hide, wait and see." Older sister no. 1: "The nuclear family lives off women's guts. Your mother has ulcers, Angela, she can't eat gravy with your daddy."

At which point Richard slapped oldest sister, his miscalculation, and she flew back to Berkeley, having cried in my hands and begged me to come with her. She missed the Sweet Sixteen party. She missed Thanksgiving and Christmas for the next two years.

Angela's jaw set hard. I saw her reject politics, feminism, and everyone's miscalculations. I hung sugar cubes from the ceiling for her party until the room looked like the picture in the magazine. I ironed sixteen pink satin ribbons she twisted in her hair. I applauded with everyone else, including the smiling halfback, when her father slipped the diamond on her finger. Then I filed for divorce.

The day Richard moved out of the house, my son switched his major to pre-med at NYU. He said it was the only way to get out of selling insurance. The last sound of the marriage was Richard being nervously sick in the kitchen sink. Angela gave him a cold washcloth and took me out to dinner at Señor Miguel's while he stacked up his boxes and drove them away. I ate chilis rellenos, guacamole chips in sour cream, cheese enchiladas, Mexican fried bread and three green chili burritos. Then I ate tranquilizers and bouillon for two weeks.

Angela was frightened.

"Mother," she said, "I wish you could be happy."

"Angela," I answered, "I'm glad you married your father, I couldn't do it anymore."

Angela finished high school the next year and twelve copies each of *Ingenue, Cosmopolitan, Mademoiselle.* She also read the Bible alone at night in her room.

"Because I'm nervous," she said, "and it helps me sleep. All the trees and fruit, the figs, begat and begat going down like the multiplication tables."

"Angela," I said, "are you thinking of making love to someone?"

"No, Mother," she said, "I think I'll wait. I think I'll wait a long time."

Angela quit eating meat and blinked her mascaraed eyes at the glistening fried liver I slid onto her plate.

"It's so brown," she said. "It's just something's guts."

"You've always loved it," I said, and she tried to eat it, glancing at my midriff, glancing at my milk and cottage cheese.

When her father took over the Midwest and married a widow, Angela declined to go with him. When I went to the hospital to have my stomach reduced by half, Angela declined my invitations to visit and went on a fast. She grew wan and romantic, said she wished I taught at her college instead of City, she'd read about Sylvia Plath in *Mademoiselle.* We talked on the telephone while I watched the hospital grounds go dark in my square window. It was summer and the trees were so heavy.

I thought about Angela, I thought about my miscalculations. I thought about milk products and white mucous coatings. About Richard's face the night of the first baby, skinny in his turned-up coat. About his mother sending roses every birth, American Beauties.

And babies slipping in the washbasin, tiny wriggling arms, the blue veins in their translucent heads. And starting oranges for ten years, piercing thick skins with a fingernail so the kids could peel them. After a while, I didn't want to watch the skin give way to the white ragged coat beneath.

Angela comes home in the summers, halfway through business, elementary education, or home ec. She doesn't want to climb the Rockies or go to India. She wants to show houses to wives, real estate, and feed me mashed potatoes, cherry pie, avocados, and artichokes. Today she not only fixes breakfast for my ex-anniversary, she fixes lunch and dinner. She wants to pile up my plate and see me eat everything. If I eat, surely something good will happen. She won't remember what's been important enough in my life to make me forget everything. She is spooning breaded clams, french fries, nuts and anchovy salad onto my plate.

"Angela, it's too much."

"That's OK, we'll save what you don't want."

"Angela, save it for who?"

She puts down her fork. "For anyone," she says. "For any time they want it."

In a moment, she slides my plate onto her empty one and begins to eat.

BLUE MOON

M y brother was a gymnast, the best in the Tri-County area; he refused to perform on any equipment but the trampoline. The trampoline was a new acquisition for Bellington High School in 1968, and Billy wanted to do things no one in Bellington had ever seen anyone do.

I didn't know I loved him deeply, not then, not yet; for days on end I had no conscious thoughts of him. After all, I was the elder sister; I was a senior, I would graduate with Honors (as honors went, in Bellington), I was pretty enough. I did right in superficial ways. I kept structures intact by attending to surfaces, trying to conceal the fact that I belonged nowhere. Uneasy, I watched Billy practice in the gym, twisting and turning as though borne up by some liquid medium.

In the weeks preceding the gym show, Billy was granted special practice time during homeroom hour. Mornings in the crowded high school, I had homeroom in the gymnasium. Thirty of us sat in one section of the portable bleachers, waiting for the scream of first-period bell. Roll was taken, announcements made. Girls gossiped. In front of us lay the basketball court, vast and blond; on the other side of it, my brother hurled himself into the air repeatedly, warming up. He was oblivious to spectators, and most only glanced at him once or twice and went back to copying homework assignments. I kept my hands open in my lap and stared at my palms, at the lines, the whorls and stars and crosses. If I looked at Billy, I wouldn't be able to look away.

I suppose Billy took up gymnastics because our mother, whose high school boyfriend had died of a heart attack after a football game, wouldn't let him play the only team sport he found glorious and interesting. He wasn't tall but his body was compact and well muscled; he could have played football. He liked the uniforms that made boys into giants, the green field progressively floodlit in the dark, the shape of the ball, the mathematical precision of the plays moving in and out of each other like animated puzzles. It didn't matter to Jean that Billy was infinitely healthy and had no heart problem. The ghost of Tom Harwin, President of the Class of '43, doctor's son, all-round hero headed for medical school, was resurrected on the three or four occasions football was reexamined as an issue; Billy was raised with the understanding that the sport was taboo. Our father, Mitch, fifteen years older than Jean, hadn't known Tom Harwin, but he allowed her this undisputed commandment as though he refused to validate her long-ago loss by arguing about it. Mitch liked football, but Bellington's passion was not his; he'd come of age in the Depression and was not a team player. He worked alone, a salesman on commission, and he let Jean's dictum stand. Billy was allowed the slow hot clockwork of baseball, the indoor bounce and jar of basketball, but he chose neither.

My brother told me he used to ask Mitch to overrule Jean about once a year; after all, Mitch was his father and football was a question of male honor and skill. Why should Jean's unreasonable fears prohibit her son a shot at the stardom she herself had valued?

I remember one discussion. Billy must have been about thirteen. We were in one of the big white Pontiacs my father owned through the years. His cars were never luxurious; they were unadorned, American, massive. It must have been summer; I remember the hum of the air-conditioner, the sighing of the vents as Mitch leaned forward to adjust the temperature. The outside world, wavering in heat lines, seemed a movie we were voyaging through, and the room of the car was a kind of inviolate space. Watching the two of them in the front seat, Billy's profile a smoother, classic version of my father's, I felt a sense of what I now know is called déjà vu—that I had watched them in just this circumstance before.

It was unsettling—even then, I didn't want to be the one who would remember everything. I wanted to physically escape the fields of feed corn fanning out from the boundaries of the two-lane road, escape the valley and the worn hills. In my memory the town stays moistly humid, green, stifled with the summer fragrance of flowering weeds. I was afraid I would watch my father and Billy speak to each other forever while the dense, mustard-bitter flowers tangled in roadside ditches. Always, my father would wear his summer hat and white, short-sleeved shirt, Billy his earnest, young face.

"Dad, I want to play. If I don't start practice as a freshman, I won't have a chance later."

Mitch looked ahead into the road and took his time answering. "Why are you so set on football?"

"Dad," he said urgently, "I want to play."

"I understand that." He waited.

"All my friends play."

"Not all of them. Some do, and some will get hurt. Oh, not hurt in ways they can't live with. I sure knocked myself around playing football, and I can't say I know why." He shifted in his seat, then sat back again, touching the leather guard on the steering wheel with one finger. "If she'd kept her mouth shut, you might never have decided you wanted it. Look, you should know that you can't talk to your mother about a damn thing. A thing is the way she sees it, and that's all. She has a certain picture in her mind, why, she can't see around it."

"Why not?" Billy raised his voice in frustration.

"She don't want to."

Billy sighed angrily. "Who was this Tom?"

Mitch shook his head. There was quiet in the car, and then he said, "Just a boy. A boy who died young."

But I wanted to know. "Dad, you don't know anything else about him?"

He looked into the rearview mirror. "Danner, hon, nothing else matters. It was twenty-five years ago."

Billy and I said nothing, unable to comprehend a quarter-century of death.

"Think of something else you want to do," Mitch said. "Something she hasn't thought of, and do that. She won't be able to stop you."

"Why not?" Billy asked.

"She just can't. She wouldn't try."

"How do I know?"

"Because I'm telling you."

"You mean you won't let her stop me?"

Mitch raised his voice again. "It's not a question of that, Billy. This thing is between you and her."

"But would you not let her?"

Mitch smiled a sort of half-grimace, turning his head to glance at me over the seat. Billy had entered a phase of life in which promises were sacred, and he exacted them at every opportunity. "All right, Billy, I wouldn't let her."

"You promised."

Mitch nodded.

Our father never had to make good on that promise. The next winter Billy started gymnastics and he got involved with Kato. For quite a while their relationship stayed as innocent as any relationship with Kato could be.

The high school hallways seemed subterranean after the brilliant daylight of the gym. Turning the corner near the water fountain I usually saw Kato, her blond hair brassy or honey-dark from one rinse or another. She gleamed, her pale blue eyes full of a flat light. If she'd grown up in a normal way, not motherless in the lawless den of her dad's pool hall, she might have been the average pretty girl, assured and not very interesting, but there was a street smarts and an urgency to her, something a little scary. She was like some high-strung animal living in a big field, always looking for cover. Billy had been a cover of sorts for over two years, despite our parents' reservations. Shinner Black, Kato's father, had been a friend of my mother's in high school; maybe that's why Jean never actually demanded Billy find himself a "nice" girl. Nice girls weren't vulnerable, and Billy seemed to have tremendous power over Kato, a whole different order of power that was partly Billy and partly something she invented for him. She often stopped me in the hall on our way to first period and talked in low tones, as though we shared the same secret but knew not to admit it. She'd pass me little gifts, a piece of gum or the kinds of chocolates and mints Shinner sold behind the bar at the pool hall, and she was always sucking on something herself, a red or green Life Saver she held between her teeth. Today she leaned close and I smelled the tart sugar of the candy. "Danner," she asked, "is Billy practicing? Did you watch?"

"Yes, he's warming up."

"Did you watch?"

"What do you mean?"

She smiled. "He says you never watch."

"Kato, I've got other things to do besides watch Billy."

"Yeah." She nodded. "Scares you, doesn't it, all these new routines he's doing."

I shrugged. "Not really. He's very exact."

"Oh, absolutely." Her face serious, she gazed off and said distractedly, as though we'd struck a bargain, "I'll go by and watch for a while. I'm failing geometry anyway." She rummaged in her purse and pressed a folded square into my hand. "Here, I wrote you a note. See you in gym."

I'd resolved not to look at Kato's notes anymore, but I couldn't help myself. She had homeroom in the library, and she sat looking at magazines in the back of the room. Evidently she thought of Billy then, and by extension, she thought of me. She gave me whole glossy pages soundlessly torn from their bindings, folded into long narrow lengths, then wrapped around themselves to form tight small squares. Each full-page advertisement (she settled for nothing less) showed people in gracious surroundings, enjoying cars, appliances, perfumes. One showed a Lincoln: a couple lounging against the car, the woman in furs, the man in formal dress. A uniformed chauffeur waited, smiling, his arm draped over the hood of the impossibly long silver car. "Me," Kato had written across his chest, and on the couple, "you and Billy." Underneath: "off for a night on the town."

Walking, I unfolded the paper. This one was a champagne ad: an oceanside terrace at sunset. A woman sat alone at a table in a diaphanous robe, touching her fluted glass; behind and below her, a couple walked along the beach, their backs to the camera, holding identical glasses. Kato had written, in block letters across the bottom, "your house!" No one was labeled and for a minute, pausing at the big trash can by the door of my soc. class, I wondered who was who. Then I folded the paper in half and threw it away quickly, as if it constituted some evidence against Kato, or maybe against me. It was as though she spoke a strange language and I understood the words against my will, but I couldn't have explained their meanings to anyone else.

Kato wasn't like the rest of us. In many ways she lived like an adult. She came and went as she pleased. She had a job—working in the pool hall making sandwiches, pouring drafts behind the bar except when the cops came in. She kept house, after a fashion, for Shinner and two older brothers, both employed now in steel mills in Ohio and seldom home. She'd never been a member of various girls' cliques around school, never a Y-Teen or Girl Scout, a delegate to Girls' Congress or church camp. Maybe it disturbed me that I'd done those things and still felt a nervous kinship with her.

She'd been an outsider, seldom spoken to by the girls in her class, teased warily by some of the boys. By virtue of her association with Billy she was no longer branded an outcast, and last summer she'd won the Miss Jaycees beauty contest. She'd borrowed a white formal of mine and entered on a dare from Billy and her father. When she won, her female compatriots at Bellington High were shocked into silence. Now she was accepted, included, even elected to the various positions high school kids invent, but she seemed to view the favor of the masses with an edgy disbelief. She knew too much to trust their change of heart.

Kato knew a lot. She knew what it was to be abandoned. A long time ago, her mother had taken off. She knew about drinking because Shinner sometimes drank. She knew about men and boys; she'd witnessed their private camaraderie and fights and gambling as a four-year-old, playing with her dolls under the pool tables. At twelve she was cooking grilled cheese sandwiches behind the bar and baking the frozen pizzas; even then, she knew about women because her dad and her brothers brought them home. She knew how to be discreet because Shinner, attractive, on the loose, occasionally got involved with someone's wife, though his visitors were more often waitresses from the truck stops. She knew how Bellington viewed her family, living over the only pool hall in town. She didn't want to know all she knew.

I wanted to know more. Last summer, in the same week Kato had triumphed in the pageant, I'd made love, twice, with an older boy from the state capital, a just-graduated senior taking courses at the local college. I liked riding down by the river in his yellow convertible. The river was steamy and brown and the trees dipped into it with the desperation of foliage choked by town dust and cinders. My friend, older, convincingly arrogant, weakened his considerable advantage over me by coming out with unbelievable, rehearsed lines like *a summer evening, a blue sky, a pretty girl.* But I liked being with him; it made me feel as though I weren't in Bellington anymore. When I said good-bye to him at summer's end like a casual friend rather than a girl who expected something, he insisted, with admiration, that I was "different." I denied it. Now I sometimes remembered the lines he'd delivered, maybe because the embarrassment I'd felt for him in those moments was a sympathy akin to love. I'd never talked to anyone about making love with him and I wondered lately if it had really happened.

Kato and Billy were lovers. Neither of them talked about it but everyone knew. Other couples cruised the streets of the town in cars, finally wrestling in backseats on some country road. Billy and Kato simply went to her house after the movies on Fridays, sports events on Saturdays, Sunday afternoons. Billy's car sat out front, parked in one of the angled spaces marked on the pavement in white paint. A door beside the pool-hall storefront led up a long narrow stairway to the Blacks' apartment.

Once I asked Billy, half kidding, what he did all those hours at the Blacks'.

"Watch TV. Play cards." He smiled.

And I believed him. They did have time to sit around like a married couple, then retire to Kato's room. Around one A.M. Billy got up, put on his clothes, and came home to make his curfew.

Maybe my mother let herself believe at first that someone was chaperoning them, but Shinner was downstairs in the pool hall, managing the peak hours of his business in a clamor of voices, cigarette smoke, jukebox music. I imagined the dull roar vibrating the floor of Kato's square white room.

"Danner? Where's your term paper?" My soc. teacher was peering down at me over her bifocals, a sheaf of papers in her hands.

I realized, fumbling through my notebook, that I'd

left the folder in the gymnasium. "Sorry," I announced, "I'll be right back."

"Just a moment," she sighed. "I'll have to give you a pass."

Walking back through the same halls I'd just negotiated, I could hear the jerky movement of the big clock on the wall. Classes murmured, and a cold wind outside blew dust around the building. It was nearly November. My mother wanted Billy to go away to a military school in January; she had a dozen brochures she'd collected through the mail, and she wanted to take Billy to see a school in Virginia as soon as the gym show was over. Billy wouldn't really discuss it but Jean kept quietly referring to his coming absence. Kato couldn't know yet—she would have asked me, questioned me, as though I could stop what was already happening.

I saw her then, standing alone at the end of the hall. She held one of the heavy gym doors open a few inches with her foot and watched Billy, her books and notebooks in a pile on the floor. She hugged herself, so rapt she didn't hear me come up behind her. She shifted her stance as she felt my presence. Silently, we watched. There were spotters now, and the coach; Billy practiced a twisting back somersault with one, then two, twists. *Stay with the doubles for now,* said the coach, but Billy did a triple. In the air, he looked like a beautiful object, hurtling end-to-end along a fall of air. He landed perfectly, knees slightly bent, both arms thrust forcefully out as though he'd suddenly become himself again.

"Danner," Kato said, "is your mother serious about sending Billy away?"

"I don't know," I lied.

She didn't quit watching; she didn't take her eyes from him. Her attentiveness, her focus, reminded me of my mother, but Jean could attend to business while the focus continued undisturbed, one clear note sounding under all her movements. She would have monitored Billy's attempted flight with an unerring third eye while maintaining a 4.0 grade point in the class Kato had discarded. Jean wanted her children to be on track, but Kato was unpredictable; she had wild yearnings and no plans.

I had plans. Maybe I was in training to become my mother, become that kind of supremely competent, unfulfilled woman, vigilant and damaged.

Kato turned to me, her eyes bright and calm. "I like to watch him," she said. "As long as I'm here, I know nothing bad can happen."

When I got home from school, my mother was sitting at the kitchen table, polishing silver. She had covered the tablecloth with a newspaper and begun with a stack of spoons. The pale salve of the polish was drying to a chalky glaze on the spoons, and my mother had lined them up in a row. The polish smelled clean and chemical, like evaporating medicine. "Hello there," she said softly.

I couldn't imagine her younger, full of helpless, specific desires, but maybe she was a refugee from those feelings. Tom Harwin had died and my mother had stayed around town, married, worked her way through college. Now she had an advanced degree and administered the county welfare office. Today she was home a little early.

She smiled up at me. "Don't ask me why I'm doing this. I suddenly thought that if I did a few pieces every day after work, I'd have finished all the silver in a week. Good therapy."

"Then maybe you and Dad should polish those spoons as a team."

My mother didn't look at me. "I don't think you're very funny," she said.

"Where is he, anyway?"

"He's downtown—where is he every day at this time?"

"I don't know. I don't know where he is when he's here."

"I can tell you that. He's sitting in the blue chair, in front of the television set."

"That's not true, Mom. Sometimes he and I are home at the same time, and I don't even know it. I hear him walking up the basement steps and realize he's been down there for hours. What does he do down there at his desk?"

My mother held a soft cotton rag in her hand as though balancing its weight. "I don't know," she said, "but whatever he does doesn't bring in much profit. I'm tired of pulling the weight for this entire family. If your father's going to spend time down there, I wish he'd do a load of wash or iron a few of his shirts."

"It's so dark and depressing in the basement," I said.

She touched the rag to a pewter-toned spoon, rubbing; it began to shine as the cloth took on a bruise of smudge. "There are lights to turn on," she said quietly. "It's not so bad. I ought to know, I sleep down there in the spare bed every night."

I nodded. "Why?"

She looked at me and lay the polished spoon at my fingers. "What do you mean, why?" Then she was silent a moment. "I can't sleep in my own bedroom. I guess I resent him lying there snoring when I'm too wrought up to close my eyes. It's dark and the house is still and I'm awake, wondering how I'm going to manage."

"Mom, you wouldn't have trouble managing if you'd forget this military-school idea."

She leaned close to me. "Listen, you must not discourage Billy from going. There's not a college in the state that'll accept him with a C-minus average. If he doesn't get into college, he'll get drafted. It's as simple as that."

"But Mom, you're sending him to a military school. It's like drafting him two years early."

"No," she said. "I know Billy. He'll buckle down and beat them at their own game. And they'll take a special interest in him, I'm sure of it."

"Right. They'll see Billy's excellent potential as cannon fodder."

My mother held one of the spoons near her face, polishing the cup of its shape. "You're wrong. Kids who go to these military prep schools are just the ones who won't go to Vietnam, unless they go as officers."

"Officers get shot, Mom. They get shot by their own men."

"Danner, will you stop?" She gave me the spoon. "Brandenburg has an excellent gymnastics team, and if Billy finishes well academically, they'll help him get a scholarship to a better school than I could ever afford." She looked into middle distance, her gaze sadly hopeful. "By the time he graduates, this war will surely be over. And the officers who teach at the school—I think Billy will find he respects these men."

"Well," I sighed, "Billy loves a worthy adversary. Why do you think he wants Kato so much?"

My mother pushed the bottle of polish to the side of the table. "I know exactly why he wants Kato. Everyone in town knows."

"That's my point, Mom. What's your real concern? Everyone in town? Why do you think Billy hasn't just refused to go? It's as though he's testing you."

"He's not testing me, he's depending on me. He's a loyal boy, and he's in over his head. What if she gets pregnant?" My mother touched my hand with hers. "It happens. People's lives get ruined."

"Maybe, but—"

Jean shook her head. "You don't know all there is to know about Kato. County welfare has had a file on that family for years, since she was a child. They had her in counseling when she was just a little girl. Of course, the way the state counseling center is run, it probably didn't do Kato much good."

"What do you mean? Counseling for what?"

"Apparently the mother drank, like Shinner, only worse. Periodically she'd put the kids in the car and drive off. She'd rent a motel room in some town and leave the kids by themselves. Finally she left them somewhere in Pennsylvania and didn't come back."

"How old was Kato?"

"Young, six or seven. Shinner wasn't around then, but his mother took the kids. She was a seamstress, lived down near the tracks. She died in just a couple of years. Shinner sold her house and bought that run-down pool hall." My mother paused, dusting each piece of the finished silver, putting each gently aside. "It's not that I have no sympathy. I was in love young; I know how it feels to pin all your hopes on someone. But Billy can't change things for a person like Kato. No matter how old he acts or how little he takes orders, he's just a kid."

I stacked the gleaming spoons carefully and put them away while she talked, one on top of the other. Their silver handles were monogrammed and bordered with delicate, minuscule leaves.

"Danner, do you have a better idea? Mitch won't discipline Billy. Brandenburg may not be the perfect solution, but it's a way to buy time." My mother looked at me levelly. "Do you really think I'm wrong?"

Two years before, Kato had gone to gymnastic meets in someone's parents' car, an unofficial, lone cheering section. The "gymnasts" in those days were a small unheralded group of boys working out on the horse and the rings. They went to a state meet as a team and placed fourth, and the school bought more equipment. Jean took her turn driving the boys to practice when they were too young to have licenses or cars. Later she drove to the meets, and Kato sat in front between Jean and Billy. Jean was amenable but she seemed to view Kato and gymnastics with the same quiet concern, maybe because both coincided with Billy's lack of interest in his grades. Jean wasn't silent about that. *You won't get into a decent college with below-average grades* or *Don't you know you'll get drafted? Vietnam is on the news every night now.*

I went along to a few of the meets. One was in Wierton, a steel town in the southern part of the state. Kato was there, looking pleased to sit beside Jean in a nearly empty gymnasium. Risers were set up the length of the floor as though for a basketball game, and the few of us in attendance felt self-conscious. Kato looked uncharacteristically proper, her hair curled and sprayed into a perfect flip. Wierton had looked gritty and deserted as we drove through the main street, and the school was dirty too. Winter sunlight fell through the high, grimy windows in beams, and motes of dust swam in the air. All the gymnastic meets seemed to be held in secret, at odd hours, early Saturday mornings or Sunday afternoons, in one deserted gym or another. There were no audiences, just the parents and a row of judges seated on folding chairs with tablets of paper in their laps. Between the routines they conferred quietly, figuring on paper. Scores were announced and marked on a blackboard. No noisy jostling among the boys waiting to perform; they sat still, concentrating, full of tension. It was a mysterious atmosphere, like the heavy silence that permeated the soundtrack of the professional-bowling show Mitch watched on Sunday television. The announcer spoke in a heavy whisper, as if the televised proceedings were forbidden. Watching Billy, I could almost hear that low, breathy male voice, commenting from somewhere beyond Kato's profile. When she looked down at her hands, her blond lashes seemed to touch her cheeks. Jean sat perfectly still, holding her purse on her knees. In front of us, Billy performed on the horse. He was a beginner and his moves must have been relatively simple; to us, they looked complicated. Balancing straight-armed on the iron pommels, he swung his legs like lethal weights, as though the lower portion of his body could be manipulated at will. There was the hard, firm slap of his hands grasping the pommels, switching off, one leg after the other scissors-kicked high and straight. He moved with clean, violent force, splicing air. Then he dismounted, and it was over.

Afterward, in the car, everyone was more relaxed. We were through Wierton quickly and on the way home.

"Kato," Jean asked, "how's your dad?"

Kato looked up. "He's fine." There was a little silence after her quick answer.

"Your dad and I were friends in high school, you know." Now that we were on the highway, Jean tried to clean the dust from the windshield. Water covered the glass as the wipers beat, clearing liquid runnels.

"I know," Kato answered. "I think my dad has pictures of you. You and him and another guy."

"Probably Tom Harwin."

"Yes, that's right. In the office, Dad has a picture in a frame. They're wearing football uniforms, and you have on, like, a fur coat?"

Jean nodded. "Chinchilla. I saved for that coat for a year, working at the soda fountain." She laughed. "I thought it was something."

"And the football helmets are funny-looking, different, smaller," Kato said. "Dad has another picture, too, over the file cabinet."

"Yes, he would. They were best friends."

"You ought to take a look, Mom." Billy put his arm lazily over the seat and touched our mother's shoulder with his hand. "Shinner's got all kinds of stuff in that office. Newspaper headlines from World War II."

"Mrs. Hampson," Kato asked, "did you know my mother?"

"No, I didn't. She wasn't from around here."

We were crossing railroad tracks and our bodies were subtly shaken by the movement of the car. Gravel crunched under the wheels. The tall caution lights, their arms crisscrossed, blinked an orange warning as we moved on.

Billy had bought a used car with money he'd saved cutting brush for the State Road Commission along the two-lanes. He'd picked Kato up every morning before school until my mother told him gently, "I don't think it's necessary to pick her up every day, as though she were family."

Sometimes I rode to school with him. The old school, where Shinner Black and Jean and Mitch had all gone, was still in operation. Country kids rode buses in from the hollows, and town kids walked or picked each other up in cars. Billy and I often passed the school bus, yellow and mottled with dust, full to overflowing, seeming to lean a bit with the grade of the pavement.

"Billy, do you and Mom ever talk about Kato?"

"No. Mom just complains to you." He grinned.

"I guess she has to complain to someone. She doesn't seem to talk to Dad much."

"No, they're not big talkers."

Town landscape flowed by. The expansive frame houses were weathered relics, their generous porches sagging. Now the outskirts of Bellington were dotted with ranch houses whose backyards melded with the long cold grasses of empty fields.

"Dad talked to me once about her, over a year ago, just a while before she and I got around to anything that needed talking about."

"He did?" I suppose my surprise showed in my voice.

Billy raised one eyebrow, his voice mischievous. "Mitch instructed me in methods of contraception. He said, 'No sense getting into a hell of a mess.' "

"That's the truth." I had to laugh at his rendition of Mitch's tone, but the story made me a little sad. I noticed my father more lately, maybe because no one else seemed to. Since he'd left his job selling cars, he spent time in the office he'd set up in the basement. He was selling aluminum buildings on commission, equipment sheds, and he was home a lot more than Jean now. I asked Billy, "Do you think Dad likes Kato?"

"Yeah, I'm sure he does. She told me he comes into the pool hall, and he always starts a conversation."

"How often does he go there?"

Billy shrugged. "Once or twice a week, in the late afternoons."

"I guess he has some time on his hands."

My brother looked over at me. "Probably so."

"What does he say about Brandenburg?"

"He doesn't say. It's Mom's money, and he's staying out of it."

"Well?"

"Well what?"

"Will you go?" He didn't answer, and I touched the cold vinyl of the car door. I could feel the vibration of the motor through it. "Don't you ever wish you could get away, anywhere, as long as it's somewhere different?"

"Not really," Billy said, "not yet. But if I went, Kato could come down and see me. I could get a part-time job down there and send her the bus fare."

"How would you have time for a job if you joined the gymnastics team?"

"I don't know. Play poker, or pool, for money. I've gotten pretty good, hanging around Shinner's." He smiled. "Don't boarding schools all have special weekends? Kato still has that white dress of yours. She could throw it in a suitcase and show up, if she could stop laughing at me in a uniform and crew cut."

"I don't think she's laughing."

We were in sight of the school and Billy slowed for the turn into the lot. "There isn't anyone like Kato," he said seriously. "I'd want to see her, no matter where I was."

I smiled back. "She's dedicated."

My brother parked his car. A necklace he'd given Kato, a gold chain, dangled from the rearview mirror. Billy turned off the ignition and sat with his hand on the keys. "I told Mom I'd go down to look at the school with her, the week after the gym show, just for three days. If I really don't like it, I'll say so, and the thing will be over. If I do, well, I think Kato will wait for me."

"When will you tell her you're going?"

"This morning."

"Be careful how you tell her."

Those last days before the gym show, the girls phys. ed. department made scenery for the requisite last number, candling to music. Entire classes of girls would move lighted candles in choreographed routines, standing, sitting, kneeling, while music played in the darkened gymnasium—easy, inclusive even of the least coordinated, impressive in simulated night. We'd practiced the movements for weeks as a simple warm-up, holding the flat glass candle holders, twisting our arms like Mata Hari's. This year we were making scenery to be spotlit to an instrumental version of "Blue Moon." "Blue moon," someone always spoofed, "I saw you hanging around. . . ." The moon was a pale blue sheet stretched over a frame; silver foil clouds would drift across on wires. Kato and I helped cut fleecy shapes from heavy cardboard. The matte knives loaned us by the art department were dull and we had to saw through the stiff board. Kato didn't meet my eyes; I knew she wouldn't mention Billy in front of the others. I was relieved when I was asked to set up folding chairs for the audience—I knew I'd finish late, after the period was over. Kato would have helped put away art supplies and gone on to another class.

Setting up stacks of metal chairs, I tried to imagine Kato next year, her senior year, without Billy. I'd be gone too, presumably to college—the thought of that unknown seemed clean and limitless, like floating in space. And Brandenburg, in the brochure Jean had shown me, seemed a universe controlled by a benevolent, all-mighty authority: the uniformed boys, the ivy-covered bell tower on the cover, couples walking under crossed sabers into a formal dance. And the gymnasts, who'd sent a member of their team to the Olympic trials, looked godly in their leotards—they were valued and privileged, they were protected. Maybe Jean was right. Walking down to the showers, I realized Billy would get away before I would. Just last night I'd noticed one of his library texts on trampolines, open on his desk to a chapter titled "Values: More Than in Any Other Activity, Trampolining Develops a Sense of Relocation."

The girls' gym facilities were identical to the boys', only smaller and painted less often. The lockers were older, battered and olive green, their catches and undependable locks installed thirty years ago. The rooms themselves were thick-walled, always damp to the touch. Painted dark green to shoulder height, they took on the pale color of the ceiling, a sour yellow reminiscent of sickness. Slanted cement floors drained into metal drains. Along the walls were the green benches where girls had sat to pull on their stockings in the forties and fifties; now we wore bright wool knee socks to match our sweaters, or fuchsia tights. The room was long and narrow, barely lit by ceiling bulbs and basement windows of dappled, frosted glass, barred with black iron. We liked to put on our skirted, dark blue gym suits and refer to ourselves as maniacs: pretense of snarls and drools as we bent to lace our tennis shoes. Empty now, the space resembled a neglected dungeon.

I walked naked into the shower room, a narrow *cul-de-sac* that smelled of mildew. The lights were badly wired and flickered. Incongruously beautiful, the shower stalls were floor-to-ceiling marble slabs, the marble a pearl white veined with gray. Their heavy doors banged, the dark paint peeling. One long horizontal mirror faced the showers over small sinks; the mirror was always cloudy, sweating, flecks of the glass gone so the surface seemed pocked with minute brown snowflakes. At the end under the windows were two toilets in wooden stalls. On their green doors someone had scratched with a nail file long ago: "No shits during showers." Just above this communication hung a more recent, official note printed by hand: DO NOT FLUSH TOILETS WHILE SHOWERS ARE RUNNING. To the right of the sign, another scrawled message: "Piss in the shower, Shit elsewhere, Good luck."

Just as I got inside and the water gurgled, bursting violently down in a hard spray, the yellow light dimmed and went out. I heard Kato come into the room, saying my name, feeling her way along the shower doors.

"Danner," she said, "is that you?"

"Yes," I answered. "Why are you still here?"

"I had to take the art supplies back upstairs."

"Kato, what happened to the light?" I reached to latch the door and touched instead Kato's cold stomach as she stepped inside.

"The bulb must be out again. Oh, make it warmer, I'm freezing."

"This is my shower," I said, "it's warm enough."

She shoved me as though in play directly under the hard warm spray and boxed her fists gently against my hands. I turned away and she moved to stand close behind me. I felt the long cool length of her body. She was laughing, and tense; she put her hands lightly on my waist and hummed a bar of "Blue Moon," then faked an openmouthed vampire kiss on my shoulder.

"You smell like Billy, do you know that?" She sighed, her voice slowed and changed. "You and Billy smell the same."

I said nothing.

"Billy's going away, isn't he? He's told you, I know he has."

"I don't know, Kato. Maybe he will."

"Shit," she whispered, like a plea, and her voice broke. She put her arms around me from behind and leaned into me with all her weight as though holding on for support.

"Kato—"

She was crying. "But he can't go. You have to tell him."

"Let go, OK?" In the warm water and the dark, I smelled the flowery musk of her wet hair. I stood still and she held on to me, swaying; I felt her face on the back of my neck, moving back and forth like the face of someone struggling in a dream. Over the running of the water I heard her ragged sobs, long sounds partially breathless, gasping. I twisted to face her and she let me but wouldn't let go. I could barely see her clenched face and I was frightened.

"Kato, please, calm down. Take a deep breath, try to breathe."

She held me, sliding down, her face on my stomach, my thighs, until she slid to her knees on the wet cement and crouched at my feet. The lights flickered then, on, off, on. I knelt beside her and she looked up at me, not really seeing me.

"Oh, God," she said, "no one will help me." She covered her face with her hands.

"I will, Kato, I will if I can. Stay here, I'll get some towels. Stay right here."

I only left her for a minute while I looked through the lockers for dry towels. When I came back she was standing in front of the mirror, the shower still running behind her. Someone had left a matte knife on the sink. Kato had the knife in her hand and she held one arm straight over her head. She watched herself in the mirror and traced a long ragged cut from her wrist to her armpit. She did it incredibly fast, with no expression, as though what she saw in the glass bore no connection to her. The little knife dropped into the sink as I reached her and she turned to me, her face stony, blood rising along the cut and pooling in the cup of her hand.

"You did the wrong thing," Billy said.

"Look, I couldn't tell then that it wasn't so bad. She was bleeding, I couldn't tell."

"You should have helped her get her clothes on and come and found me."

"Billy, if the cut had been deeper she could have bled to death while I was looking for you."

"But it wasn't so deep." Above him, Jean's kitchen

clock ticked like a mechanical heartbeat. Finally, it was dark and the day was over. Billy shook his head. "Did she mean it to be worse?"

"I don't know. The knife was dull and she couldn't press hard, the way she held her arm. But she cut herself. She had thirty stitches. When I found you, Billy, what would you have done? Sewn up her arm? Oh, you have to let other people help now."

He didn't answer, his hands flat on the surface of the oak table. They hadn't let him see her at the hospital, but later, when she went home with her father, he'd been there, waiting for hours.

"Billy, what did she say to you?"

"She was in her room, lying down. She made light of it, said they gave her free Valium, and she's going to visit her aunt in Ohio. She said Dayton wasn't New York City but it's bigger than Bellington." His voice dropped. "She said she was sorry."

"Did you talk to Shinner?"

Billy nodded. "He said not to stay because of Kato, that she'd be with his sister until Christmas, maybe the whole school year. That we could write and talk but there should be distance."

"Billy," I said, "maybe he's right."

He looked, bewildered, into the air, his eyes wet. "I told her I was just going down to look. That's all, take a look."

The gymnastics show occurred on schedule, two days later, on a cold Friday night. Kato had been sent to Ohio to her relatives and Billy had canceled his performance on the trampoline. I went to the show only because I couldn't face staying home with Jean and Mitch, and Billy in his room in silence, his suitcase packed. My father drove me to the school and I walked through various routines with my classes, but toward the end I couldn't face the last number, the candling maneuvers to "Blue Moon" in darkness. I didn't want to see a hundred girls moving flames in patterns, shadows passing over the homemade moon.

I made my way outside and stood by the big double doors of the school. Boys from the country stood out there—the ones who wore boots and hunting caps with earflaps, and torn, fleece-lined leather jackets. One of them offered me a cigarette. We stood, smoking, and I watched them. What made sense? This moment was real. In some other instance these four boys might sneer at me, as they often sneered, threateningly, at girls from town. Or they might attack me. Why was the world one thing and not another?

I stood breathing the cold air, smelling the stark, clean cold. The boys jostled each other, drinking from a flask, and filed slowly out into the dark. They walked toward a pickup truck parked in the high school lot, where they could drink without fear of discovery. I watched them go and looked into the darkness in front of me, into the circular, empty drive of the school and the highway beyond.

A man walked unsteadily toward me out of the snow.

I wasn't afraid of him; I felt a solidarity with all outcasts. I wasn't supposed to have to wrap bleeding girls in towels, or walk us both half naked into a school hallway for help. I wasn't supposed to smoke cigarettes with country boys, or smoke cigarettes in the light where anyone could see, or even stand in the snow in a skimpy gym suit, shivering. Besides, I recognized the man by his thick, broad shoulders, and the set of his body. He came nearer and stopped opposite me. It was Kato's father.

Shinner Black weaved slightly in the dark. He stood with legs spread and might have sunk slowly into one of the graceful gymnast's splits I'd seen inside. "I knew your mother in high school," he said to me.

I moved a little, stepping back toward the shelter of the building. "Maybe you'd better stand against this wall here," I said.

He brought his feet together, straightened, and walked two steps closer. "Did you hear me?" he asked softly.

His voice was melodic. Despite the haze of his drunkenness, he seemed informed by some wonder and looked carefully at me. Now he stood in the light as the snow fell behind him, and I saw in his face the smooth, shadowed face of the boy in my mother's scrapbook photographs. He sensed my surprise and my apprehension; his light eyes were unfocused but oddly alert, the eyes of a person hypnotized rather than blearily drunk. He searched my face with his distant gaze, as though looking for another face beneath my features.

"I was Tom Harwin's best friend," he said. "After that summer, I joined the army." He stared off into the weather, then jerked his head as if something had occurred to him. "You know who I mean? Tom. Your mother's beau, Tom and Jean."

"Yes, I know."

He came suddenly close, bent forward as though he were falling. Reflexively, I put my hands up to stop him. He leaned heavily against me at arm's length, his chest against the palms of my hands. His coat was open. I felt the warmth of his skin through the thin fabric of his shirt, and the vibrations of his voice.

"You should have seen this town then," he said, looking at the ground. "We had a good time the year before he died. Everyone was gone to the war. We high school boys, we were the men of the town."

To keep my own balance, I had to lean slightly toward him. "Mr. Black," I said. Across the parking lot, I saw the boys pause in the passing of their flask and stand watching us.

"I found out better," Shinner Black said. "In the war, in France, nobody even spoke English. That was a joke we had."

I waited, then he smiled and seemed to regain his balance. He stood, his face inches from mine, and put his hands on my shoulders. He held me so tightly I felt the pressure of each of his fingers. "People can't live in this world," he said. His voice was furious and tender; I felt the supportive, viselike grip of his hands and an unfamiliar, charged dizziness. The pressure of his grasp seemed to lift me toward him and I didn't resist. I moved my hands in confusion and inadvertently touched his warm throat. We stood totally alone in the snow, and the space in which we stood seemed to turn in unhurried, resolute circles. What remained outside —the walls of the building behind us, the white ground and the highway, the parking lot and the boys, who yelled Shinner's name once, twice—blurred and receded. Shinner's hands relaxed their hard grip and he still held me, near him. We stood motionless.

I must have looked terrified. The boys had begun walking toward us; when they were close enough to see my face, they broke into a loping run across the powdery lawn. Their dark forms were silhouettes in the quiet snow. Someone's shoulder jarred my face as he moved to stand between Shinner and me; the cold leather of his jacket was against my eyes and smelled of smoke. The boys themselves smelled dirty, oddly sweet, like urine, and the open flask had spilled on someone's sleeve. Suddenly the clear cold was full of commotion. The boys surrounded Shinner as though to protect him and began to pull him away; one of them trod heavily on my feet and left the print of his boot on my canvas shoes. Excluded by the jostling of their big bodies, I understood they were saving Shinner, not me. "I'm sorry," I said to no one. Shinner didn't look back and the boys led him quickly toward the truck; one of them waved me away good-naturedly.

As they moved off into the snow, a blur of arms and broad backs, I saw my father's big Pontiac turn into the half-moon drive of the school. The car slid as he braked too sharply and slowed to a stop. Across a small sea of weather and darkness, the white car sat like a gleaming boat, headlights throwing their long beams into the slant of the snow. The snow was turning to rain. My father put the car in parking gear as he opened the door and the interior light clicked on. Inside this small, lit room I saw the familiar movement of his shoulders, his gloved hands. He pushed the heavy door of the car quickly open, and half stood in the drive, one hand still on the wheel. His questioning face was in shadow, lit from below by the dim yellowed light of the car.

I raised my hand to tell him everything was all right, to wait while I went inside for my coat, but he misunderstood and walked over toward me. His boot buckles jangled with every footfall and the abandoned Pontiac buzzed, the keys still in the ignition.

"What the hell is going on here?" my father asked when he reached me.

"Nothing. I came out for some air and he was here, talking to himself."

"Who was here? Who was that?" Mitch looked after them into the parking lot.

"Mr. Black, Kato's father."

"You mean Shinner Black?" My father shook his head, half in sympathy. "Christ," he said.

A gust of wind peppered us with sharp snowy rain and my father pulled his hat down over his eyes. I was trembling but I wasn't cold. A slow warmth had eased through me.

"What are you doing in the cold with nothing on?"

Mitch said. "Go get your coat. I'll wait right here in the car."

He hunched his shoulders and moved back into the rain as I turned and felt for the cold knob of the heavy door. It pushed open easily, as though pulled from within by the crowded warmth and bright fluorescence of the gymnasium. I could hear cheers; the girls were beginning candling maneuvers and the loudspeaker system crackled air. The lights went dim. I got my coat from my locker and watched by the gym door. They stood in formation, the candles two hundred lights in the dark, and stereo speakers released the melody: Blue moon, I saw you standing alone. Flames circled and dipped as the spotlight lit the crescent we'd cut from a sheet and stretched across a wood frame. The silver foil clouds moved on dependable wires, gliding slowly across the face of the moon.

Monday morning I stood on the corner near our house, waiting for the school bus. In my pocket I had a letter to Kato from Billy—Shinner would send it to her. I didn't want to go to school, and the pool hall would be empty now. Abruptly, I turned and walked down the hill into town. It was a bright winter morning, snow thawing to slush. I could hear gutter water flowing in the street drains, a sound loud and close up and fresh. The air felt like early spring, as though everything had emptied, lightened and warmed, because Billy and Kato were gone.

Before I got to the pool hall, I could see Shinner's truck parked in front. Evidence of his presence gave me pause, but I kept walking. If my nerve failed I could just pass by, walk past the movie theater onto Main Street. But I crossed, touched the chrome bumper of the Chevy truck, and walked up the steps of the hall. Through the storefront window I saw Shinner at the bar, smoking and looking at notebooks. His expression was serious and he looked the picture of normalcy: a man at work. If I'd found him in the same state in which he'd appeared to me the night of the storm, a kind of apparition that canceled everything else, I'd have felt more confident. I knocked on the steel door and heard him walk over. The door opened.

"I'm Billy's sister," I said, as though he wouldn't remember.

He stepped back to let me enter. "Billy get off OK?"

"Yes. Yesterday morning." I followed him across the big room to the bar. The hall was empty, the tables covered with plastic cloths. The notebooks were account ledgers, full of figures. Beside them sat an ashtray full of butts and a Styrofoam cup of coffee.

"Want some coffee?" He moved behind the bar to pour it before I could answer, then set a steaming cup in front of me. "I don't have any milk, just these things." He pushed forward a basket of creams packaged in individual plastic cups. "Half-and-half, pretty fancy."

"I have something for Kato," I said quickly. "A letter from Billy. He said you would send it to her."

He shook his head. "Not yet. You keep it. In a week or so, I'll call and give you the address."

I nodded. We sat awkwardly, looking at the cup and its dark liquid.

"I'm sorry about the other night," he said quietly. "I'm sorry if I scared you."

"That's OK." I turned to face him. He sat, just watching me, in his dark green flannel shirt with the cigarette pack in the pocket. His forearms were muscular. His features were strong and regular but he looked almost as old as my father, handsome and ruined. His pants were a little too short and he wore white athletic socks and sneakers. I saw every detail of him, the way he looked.

"I sent Kato to my sister," he said. "It's good they're apart. She did it to keep Billy from leaving, but if he'd stayed, what would that tell her?"

I wasn't sure, so I didn't answer.

"Everyone so shocked," he said, looking into the room, "like kids don't know enough to be that serious. Hell, that's when it happens." He paused. "And she did it in front of you."

His voice was full of sorrow. Again, I wondered if I was somehow culpable. She was trying to influence Billy, not me; why hadn't she done it in front of him? Regardless, she had Billy now—he would not outdistance her, if he tried to, no more than my mother had moved past Tom Harwin. And I was witness, connected to her; the boundary I'd imagined between myself and anything I saw or touched, was gone. Everything was different now, larger, enveloped by a shadow. Shinner Black was silent, waiting as my thoughts fell against each other like a long line of dominoes. It felt as though my vision had altered, as though I'd seen things through a dull filter that now disintegrated.

Shinner Black moved his hand across the bar and touched my wrist. "It feels like the world has ended," he said. "But you kids are not like us. You won't always live here. Already, you're practically gone."

I looked away from him, at the wall behind the bar, and my gaze fell on an eight-by-ten glossy of Kato, the picture that had been in the papers last summer when she'd won the pageant. Even now, the Scotch tape that held it to the plaster was yellowed.

BESS

*Y*ou have to imagine: this was sixty, seventy, eighty years ago, more than the lifetimes alloted most persons. *Lord save us,* is what we used to say—we younger ones—as an expression, sometimes in jest. Later I said it in earnest, in the long winters, light in the rooms so dim and the rooms themselves like shadowy caves. Some months we children took lessons at home, as Coalton was thirty minutes wagon ride and snow too deep for the wheels; drifts on the road were waist-high. Pa did have a sledge but traveled any distance only in emergency. A few times, in a snap freeze, the snow grew shiny and hard, gleaming as though a mirror were shattered across its whole surface. Pa marked a track with sticks and bundled us in furs. We rode round, runners of the sledge tracing a circle past the house and the naked oaks. The belled harness jingled and beyond the oaks were fields on all sides, sloping flat to the woods. We were warned not to go out of track. Further out the snow was soft in spots and would swallow us right up, Pa said. This was probably only a story, though we lost an animal nearly every winter, in just that way—goats or hogs lost in a drift, frozen perfectly until a thaw revealed them.

From the age of eight or nine, my brother Warwick drove the sledge. We sisters sat wrapped together in blankets and the bear rug, our faces covered except for our eyes. Warwick sat forward with the whip and reins, making the horse step quickly to stay warm. Pa followed on snowshoes; behind us he looked like a bulky troll against the white, which fairly glinted like a glassy sea with slopes. The circle, round the big house and the empty guesthouse, was perhaps a half-mile. Warwick whistled and shouted to the horse, his voice high-pitched, a child's voice floating out and freezing. It was like flying, slicing through the wind with the air so cold we couldn't see into it.

Finally Warwick let us off by the big porch that was heaped with snow, then drove the sledge to the barn where Pa met him. We sisters went in to the fire, all of us shining with cold, and the fire warmed us, turned us one by one to our winter selves, dim in the dim house, the windows all shuttered against the cold, the lamps throwing off small glows.

Our parents joked about their two families, first the six sons, one after the other; then a few years later the four daughters, Warwick, and me. Another daughter after the boy was a bad sign, Pa said; there were enough children. I was the last, youngest of twelve Hampsons, and just thirteen months younger than Warwick. Since we were born on each other's heels, Mam said, we would have to raise each other.

Warwick, Ava, and I shared one room, the three other sisters another. In winter only the big kitchen was kept truly warm. It was considered dangerous to have wood stoves or coal burners in children's bedrooms; we slept under feather comforters, close to each other. Ava was four years older and often appointed to watch Warwick and me. She longed for the company of the older sisters and yet took a kind of pride in her responsibility. I remember her teaching us, with chalks on a slate, gravely, the letter *S*. I was not even talking yet; she taught me to hiss, then drew one line and changed the *S* to an *8*. *S, 8*. Something was flickering all around us. Doubtless it was the fire, lit on a winter evening when the dark came so early. I remember no one's face, but I see her hand on the slate beside the magic form. Those long winters inside were not bad times at first, but in later weeks a strange loneliness came—late in the cold, the last few weeks before it broke, we seldom talked or read aloud or argued anymore, or played games. We lived instead in silence, only doing what we were told to do, and waiting.

We could see no other farms from our house, not a habitation or the smoke of someone's chimney; we could not see the borders of the road anymore but only the cover of snow, the white fields, and mountains beyond. The mountains were an awesome height; you could not see where the sky began. The house in this whiteness seemed small, alien, as though we might be covered up and vanish; no one would know. Sounds were so muffled; except for the wind, one could have fantasies of deafness. The power of the Scriptures in such a setting was great and we heard the

Bible aloud nearly every evening. Twilight, because the valley was deep, came as early as three or four in the afternoon; the world, the snow, seemed to fly in the face of the Word. *Remove not the old landmarks, venture not into the fields of the fatherless;* yet the snow still fell.

Winters frightened me, but it was summers I should have feared. Summers, when the house was large and full, the work out-of-doors so it seemed no work at all, everything done in company. Summers all the men were home, the farm was crowded, lively; it seemed nothing could go wrong then.

The six elder brothers had all left home at sixteen to homestead somewhere on the land, each going first to live with the brother established before him. They worked mines or cut timber for money to start farms and had an eye for women who were not delicate. Once each spring they were all back to plant garden with Pa, and the sisters talked amongst themselves about each one. All older than the girls and distant enough to be mysteries, they were comely men and this week alone appeared all together without their wives, filling the house after the long silent winter and taking hours to eat big suppers the sisters served after nightfall.

Noons we took turns carrying water to them on horseback, corked bottles we'd filled in the cold creek. We sat astride and they drank at our knees. Each had a favorite sister; they were a bit shy when alone with the one they liked most. Sometimes there was an awkward silence while they drank. They were strong men; they were all alive then. To think of them, drinking cold water and sweating, squinting against the sun at a face.

By late June the brothers had brought their families, each a wife and several children. All the rooms in the big house were used, the guesthouse as well, swept and cleaned. There was always enough space because each family lived in two big rooms, one given to parents and youngest baby and the other left for older children to sleep together, all fallen uncovered across a wide cob-stuffed mattress. Within those houses were many children, fifteen, twenty, more. I am speaking now of the summer I was twelve, the summer Warwick got sick and everything changed.

He was nearly fourteen. We slept in the big house in our same room but chose favorite cousins to share the space, as the four elder sisters in summer had their own two rooms over the sun porch, open to river breeze; they were all young ladies now and I had little to do with them. Ava told me I was more a boy than a girl. I didn't care; the young cousins all wanted to be chosen, as our room was bay-windowed, very large, and directly above the parlor, the huge oak tree lifting so close our window it was possible to climb out at night and sit hidden on the branches. Adults on the porch were different from high up, the porch lit in the dark and chairs creaking as the men leaned and rocked, murmuring, drinking homemade beer kept cool in cellar crocks.

Late one night that summer, Warwick woke me, pinched my arms inside my cotton shift and held his hand across my mouth. He walked like a shadow in his white nightclothes, motioning I should follow him outside; I could see his clothes and not his body in the dark. Warwick was quickly through and I was slower, my weight still on the sill as he settled himself, then lifted me over when I grabbed a higher branch, my feet on his chest and shoulders. We climbed into the top branches that grew next the third floor of the house and sat cradled where three branches sloped; Warwick whispered not to move, stay behind the leaves in case they look. We were outside Claude's window, seeing into the dim room.

Claude was youngest of the older brothers and his wife was hugely with child, standing like a white column in the middle of the floor. Her white chemise hung wide round her like a tent and her sleeves were long and belled; she stood, both hands pressed to the small of her back, leaning as though to help the weight at her front. Then I saw Claude kneeling, darker than she because he wasn't wearing clothes. He touched her feet and I thought at first he was helping her take off her shoes, as I helped the young children in the evenings. But he had nothing in his hands and was lifting the thin chemise above her knees, higher to her thighs, then above her hips as she was twisting away but stopped and moved more toward him, only holding the cloth bunched to conceal her belly. She pressed his head away from her, the chemise pulled to her waist in back and his one hand there trying to hold her. Then he backed her three steps to the foot of the bed and she half leaned, knees just bent; he knelt down again, his face almost at her feet and his mouth moving like he was biting her along her legs. She held him just away with her hands and he touched over and over the big globed belly, stroking it long and deeply like you would stroke a scared animal. Suddenly he held her at her knees and tipped her whole body back, moved her thighs apart, and was right up against her with his face, eating: it looked backwards and terrible, like a big crouched cat suckling its smaller mother— she leaning back totally now with both hands over her mouth. Then he stood quickly and turned her so her belly was against the heaped sheets. She grasped the bed frame with both hands so when he pulled her hips close she was bent prone forward from the waist; now her hands were occupied and he uncovered all of her, pushing the chemise to her shoulders and past her breasts in front; the filmy cloth hid her head and face, falling even off her shoulders so it hung halfway down her arms. She was all naked globes and curves, head-less and wide-hipped with the swollen belly big and pale beneath her like a moon; standing that way she looked all dumb and animal like our white mare before she foaled. All this time she was whimpering, Claude looking at her. We saw him, he started to prod himself inside her very slow, tilting his head and listening. . . . I put my cool hands over my eyes then, hearing their sounds until Warwick pulled my arms down and made me look. Claude was tight behind her, pushing in and flinching like he couldn't get out of her; she bawled once. He let her go, stumbling; they staggered onto the bed, she lying on her back away from him with the bunched chemise in her mouth. He pulled her to him and took the cloth from her lips and wiped her face.

This was perhaps twenty minutes of a night in July, 1900. I looked at Warwick as though for the first time. When he talked he was so close I could feel the words on my skin distinct from night breeze. "Are you glad you saw?" he whispered, his face frightened.

He had been watching them from the tree for several weeks.

"Warwick. Warwick, are you here?"

Thick wide door of the barn shuts behind me; inside it is darker than morning in the field, where the light seems nearly ivory, indirect and still diffuse, early. Inside, the barn is a color nearly olive, furred with warmth and the smells of animals close all night. Coolness come finally just at dawn is only barely felt. Morning, early morning, as the Independence Day parade begins at noon in Coalton and we have both horses to curry and brush.

"Warwick, you have the ribbon? I brought the satin but the rest was gone from the sewing box."

He says, "I have the grosgrain, there, in the basket."

Now I hear Mags and Race, snorting in the far stalls at the end and Warwick is there. I don't see the combs, the silver shine in his hands, but hear their teeth on the horses' long necks and see Warwick. Both arms moving smooth and repetitive as in some purposeful dance except all his body is still, just standing, while his arms stay lifted, stroking. He watches his hands, the combs, and the horses whinny because I'm closer and they smell apples.

"Ava is making the carriage streamers," I tell him.

The apples are in my apron and I reach for them, not looking; they're hard and small and sweet; the horses jostle and lower their long heads to mouth my palm with their velvety lips that leave no wetness. There is the sound of the apples cracking and the big breathing of horses. Warwick steps back. There are the combs in his palms, their leather straps across the backs of his hands.

"Are the rest of them awake?" he asks.

"Yes, up cooking food for the picnic. Where did you sleep?"

"Out here."

He touches my shoulder with the side of his wrist and his face is still in half-shadow. While he talks my eyes get used to the dimness and I see his mouth, the line of his jaw. He has a thin, narrow face that is sensitive and changing; already he is a head taller than me.

"You didn't mean to watch them," he says. "I led you into it. You won't tell anyone?"

"No. But if you watch them again I don't want to know."

"I won't watch them. Here, take the grosgrain first. You do Mags."

He puts the combs down where they glint in straw and we prop the basket of ribbons between us, against the stall. The horses stand very still, almost somnolent, while we touch them. Our fingers in their long

manes are plaiting the rough hair, the hair coarse and
cool and dead against the warmth of their broad necks.
In the quiet the horses feel big and human, their hard
heads pressed close our shoulders.

"You remember when Claude got married?" Warwick says.

His hands are faster; he knots the red grosgrain into
each plait and crosses thin ribbons, red, blue, down
each length to keep the braids tight. Mags and Race
stay still, only shifting their weight and moving hind-
quarters to stand where the straw is thicker.

"I remember, we all went down to Bluefield on the
train. Was it two years ago?"

"She was in a family way. Then, at the wedding."

"How would you know?"

"Claude told me. He said she was, and he had made
it right to her and did not regret it. She lost that baby
early on and felt badly, like he had married her now
for no reason—but Claude said he would have anyway,
got married, because he was her first."

"Her first?"

"Yes, he knew he was. He was her first and a woman
belongs to that man, whether she is with him later or
not."

"I don't believe you, Warwick. What about the
Jones girl, the one hurt last spring by that tramp?"

He touches Race under her mane, pulls a lock of the
coarse hair straight.

"Well?" I ask him.

"The tramp was lynched, wasn't he? If the girl had
been a tramp herself, the man would have been let go
or jailed. But she was young and her father dead and
her brothers not grown, so the townsmen met in Coalton and found the man."

"But the tramp can't own her when he's dead. Who
owns her then?"

Warwick is still a moment in the shady light, his

hands moving, and between us the basket is nearly empty. The straw bottom looks white in this dimness.

"I don't know," he says. "I guess then she's a kind of orphan."

The satin ribbon is knotted in a coil beneath grosgrain, slick and silky by the nubby darker red—unrolling it I feel the basket shift and almost fall. Warwick catches it, kneeling down beside me to hold it with one hand.

"But a woman does belong to her first man and that is the truth," he says.

"I think it's a lie."

"How do you mean?"

"I know, I know it is."

"How can you know?"

"I feel it, I'm certain."

"You feel it because you don't know."

In old photographs of Coalton that July 4th, the town looks scruffy and blurred. The blue of the sky is not shown in those black-and-white studies, nor the colors of the streamered buildings and the flags, the finery worn by the crowd. Wooden sidewalks on the two main streets were broad and raised; that day people sat along them as on low benches, their feet in the dusty road, waiting for the parade. We were all asked to stay still as a photographer took pictures of the whole scene from a near hillside. People did sit quite still, or stand in place, some of them in windows of the old hotel; then there was a prayer blessing the new century and the cornet band assembled. The parade was forming out of sight, by the river, and most townspeople driving decorated carriages had already driven out—Warwick had gone, with Claude and Pa, and some of the young cousins. It would be a big parade; we had word that local merchants had hired part of a circus traveling through Bellington. I ran up the hill to

see if I could get a glimpse of them; Mam was calling
me to come back and my shoes were blond to the
ankles with dust. Below me the crowd began to cheer.
The ribboned horses danced with fright and kicked,
jerking reins looped over low branches of trees and
shivering the leaves. From up the hill I saw dust raised
in the woods and heard the crackling of what was
crushed. There were five elephants; they came out
from the trees along the road and the trainer sat on the
massive harnessed head of the first. He sat in a sort of
purple chair, swaying side to side with the lumbering
swivel of the head. The trainer wore a red cap and
jacket; he was dark and smooth on his face and held
a boy close his waist. The boy was moving his arms at
me and it was Warwick; I was running closer and the
trainer beat with his staff on the shoulders of the elephant while the animal's snaky trunk, all alive, ripped
small bushes. Warwick waved; I could see him and ran,
dodging the men until I was alongside. The earth was
pounding and the animal was big like a breathing wall,
its rough side crusted with dirt and straw. The skin
hung loose, draped on the limbs like sacking crossed
with many creases. Far, far up, I saw Warwick's face;
I was yelling, yelling for them to stop, stop and take
me up, but they kept on going. As the elephants
passed, dust lifted, and ribbons and hats, the white of
the summer skirts swung and billowed. The cheering
was a great noise under the trees and birds flew up
wild. Coalton was a sea of yellow dust, the flags snap-
ping in that wind and banners strung between the
buildings broken, flying.

Warwick got it in his head to walk a wire and none
could dissuade him. Our Pa would not hear of such
foolishness so Warwick took out secretly to the creek
every morning and practiced on the sly. He con-
structed a thickness of barn boards lengthwise on the

ground, propped with nailed supports so he could walk along an edge. First three boards, then two, then one. He walked barefoot tensing his long toes and cradled a bamboo fishing pole in his arms for balance. I followed along silently when I saw him light out for the woods. Standing back a hundred feet from the creek bed, I saw through dense summer leaves my brother totter magically just above the groundline; thick ivy concealed the edges of the boards and made him appear a jerky magician. He often walked naked since the heat was fierce and his trousers too-large hand-me-downs that obstructed careful movement. He walked parallel to the creek and slipped often. Periodically he grew frustrated and jumped cursing into the muddy water. Creek bottom at that spot was soft mud and the water perhaps five feet deep; he floated belly-up like a seal and then crawled up the bank mud-streaked to start again. I stood in the leaves. He was tall and still coltish then, dark from the sun on most of his body, long-muscled; his legs looked firm and strong and a bit too long for him, his buttocks were tight and white. It was not his nakedness that moved me to stay hidden, barely breathing lest he hear the snap of a twig and discover me—it was the way he touched the long yellow pole, first holding it close, then opening his arms gently as the pole rolled across his flat still wrists to his hands; another movement, higher, and the pole balanced like a visible thin line on the tips of his fingers. It vibrated as though quivering with a sound. Then he clasped it lightly and the pole turned horizontally with a half-rotation; six, seven, eight quick flashes, turning hard and quick, whistle of air, snap of the light wood against his palms. Now the pole lifted, airborne a split second and suddenly standing, earthward end walking Warwick's palm. He moved, watching the sky and a wavering six feet of yellow needle. The earth stopped in just that moment, the trees still, Warwick moving, and then as the pole toppled in a smooth arc to water he followed in a sideways dive. While he was under, out of earshot and rapturous in the olive water, I ran quick and silent back to the house, through forest and vines to the clearing, the meadow, the fenced boundaries of the high-grown yard and the house, the barn, where it was shady and cool and I could sit in the mow to remember his face and the yellow pole come to life. You had to look straight into the sun to see its airborne end and the sun was a blind white burn the pole could touch. Like Warwick was prodding the sun in secret, his whole body a prayer partly evil.

That night I saw our mother hold his feet in her lap. She ran the cold edge of her steel darning needle up and down, up and down his flesh, taking painlessly the splinters from his skin. I stood with a lamp, hidden from sight at the porch door; beyond the filtered light of the globe close my face I saw my brother, my mother, two lumps in pale garments, moving, and past them the foreshortened planks of porch floor shaded a graduated dark. The round porch pillars were lost at one fat end in eaves. Low grass of the yard rumpled like carpet to the fence, pickets waist-high and blurred at field's edge. Out there the dogs bayed long-drawn howls, scouting near the creek for coons while dusk held. The dogs moved in a pack, eyes squinted near shut in the high sharp grass.

The sky those summer nights was like the pale inside of an overturned blue bowl, blue and light longer than the earth or the fields were light. Fireflies blinked in the tall black grass while it was still nearly daytime. Close by, crickets made a shrill weeping under the house; cats slid, hunting; Warwick called our mother "Mam" and she touched his feet, silent, Warwick looking away across the yard. Meadows had lost definition.

Breeze wavered the whole slow mass like deep water and made a sound, a sighing pitched low and perfect: I was standing with the lamp in my hand and thought the house moved beneath my feet, slipped and slid with a creaking like a ship, like we were all afloat. The wick in the lamp flared up then, the fire leaped in the globe. As though in reply the wind murmured loud beyond the wheat and the grasses, far out in the woods. Mam and Warwick sat still, their heads lifted, listening.

Suddenly I was ashamed and blew out the light lest they know I watched them. I lowered my eyes and gazed at my own feet until I saw clearly their white shapes on the floor. When I looked again, Mam had turned her back to him. He sat leaning against the broad porch column, long legs extended so he braced her back with his feet, and then he moved, slowly, one foot flat to the base of her spine and the other higher, nearly to the blades of her shoulders; and so he bent his knees and rocked her, both of them quiet; he took all her weight and rocked her with his legs as though she were in those long full skirts some voluminous silent object. All this in silence but for a creaking of boards as her weight shifted.

Stubborn as the devil's agent, she called him, but she was partial to her male children and Warwick was the youngest of the boys. She allowed disobedience from none but him; he was always wild and taken with strange notions. Born that way and encouraged too by his position in the family: next-to-last of twelve, largely overlooked by the older brothers and easy victor over sisters closer his age. He was good at shenanigans and saved himself many a cuff or belting by a witticism at the right moment. Regardless, he didn't care if he was hit and never altered his behavior due to any punishment. *Deliver my soul from the sword,* we read for summer lessons, Warwick halting and angry at being inside the warm kitchen, *and my darling from the power of the dog.* His eyes were long-lashed and narrow, yellow-brown, lightened with bright slashes the color of copper; he squinted sideways at me and touched big Malantha, the fat hound, with his feet, shoving her secretly toward me under the table so she woke and yawned with my whole foot wet in her big jowled mouth.

One day, of course, he saw me watching him practice, and knew in an instant I had watched him all along; by then he was actually walking a thick rope strung about six feet off the ground between two trees. For a week he'd walked only to a midpoint, as he could not rig the rope so it didn't sag and walking all the way across required balance on the upward slant. That day he did it; I believe he did it only that once, straight across. I made no sound but as he stood there poised above me his eyes fell upon my face; I had knelt in the forest cover and was watching as he himself had taught me to watch. Perhaps this explains his anger—I see still, again and again, Warwick jumping down from the rope, bending his knees to an impact as dust clouds his feet but losing no balance, no stride, leaping toward me at a run. His arms are still spread, hands palm-down as though for support in the air, and then I hear rather than see him because I'm running, terrified— shouting his name in supplication through the woods as he follows, still coming after me wild with rage as I'd never seen anyone. Then I was nearly out of breath and just screaming, stumbling—

It's true I led him to the thicket, but I had no idea where I was going. We never went there as it was near a rocky outcropping where copperheads bred, and not really a thicket at all but a small apple orchard gone diseased and long dead. The trees were oddly dwarfed and broken, and the ground cover thick with vines.

Just as Warwick caught me I looked to see those rows of small dead trees; then we were fighting on the ground, rolling. I fought with him in earnest and scratched his eyes; already he was covered all over with small cuts from running through the briers. This partially explains how quickly he was poisoned, but the acute nature of the infection was in his blood itself. Now he would be diagnosed severely allergic and given antibiotics; then we knew nothing of such medicines. The sick were still bled. In the week he was most ill, Warwick was bled twice daily, into a bowl. The doctor theorized, correctly, that the poison had worsened so as to render the patient's blood toxic.

Later Warwick told me, if only I'd stopped yelling— Now that chase seems a comical as well as nightmarish picture; he was only a naked enraged boy. But the change I saw in his face, that moment he realized my presence, foretold everything. Whatever we did from then on was attempted escape from the fact of the future.

"Warwick? Warwick?"

The narrow sun porch is all windows but for the house wall. He sleeps here like a pupa, larva wrapped in a woven spit of gauze and never turning. His legs weeping in the loose bandages, he smells of clear fluid seeped from wounds. The seepage clear as tears, clear as sweat but sticky on my hands when my own sweat never sticks but drips from my forehead onto his flat stomach, where he says it stings like salt.

"Warwick. Mam says to turn you now."

Touching the wide gauze strips in the dark. His ankles propped on rolls of cloth so his legs air and the blisters scab after they break and weep. The loose gauze strips are damp when I unwrap them, just faintly damp; now we don't think he is going to die.

He says, "Are they all asleep inside?"

"Yes. Except Mam woke me."

"Can't you open the windows? Don't flies stop when there's dew?"

"Yes, but the mosquitoes. I can put the netting down but you'll have that dream again."

"Put it down but come inside, then I'll stay awake."

"You shouldn't, you should sleep."

Above him the net is a canopy strung on line, rolled up all the way round and tied with cord like a bedroll. It floats above him in the dark like a cloud the shape of the bed. We keep it rolled up all the time now since the bandages are off his eyes; he says looking through it makes everyone a ghost and fools him into thinking he's still blind. Before, he didn't know the difference and so the netting was down and the room cooler, breeze through all the open windows helped him heal. That was night. Days the doctor told us to keep the windows shut so sun poured through the glass panes, dried the blisters and new rash. So hot Ava stood and fanned him with Mam's big palm fan, while I was the only one allowed to touch him because I don't catch poison.

Now I stand on a chair to reach the knotted cords, find them by feel, then the netting falls all around him like a skirt.

"All right, Warwick, see me? I just have to unlatch the windows."

Throw the hooks and windows swing outward all along the sun-porch walls. The cool comes in, the lilac scent, and now I have to move everywhere in the dark because Mam says I can't use the lamp, have kerosene near the netting.

"I can see you better now," he says from the bed.

I can tell the shadows, shapes of the bed, the medicine table, the chair beside him where I slept the first nights we moved him to the sun porch. Doctor said he'd never seen such a poison, Warwick's eyes swollen shut, his legs too big for pants, soles of his feet oozing in one straight seam like someone cut them with scissors. Mam with him day and night until her hands broke out and swelled; then it was only me, wrapping him in bandages she cut and rolled wearing gloves.

"Let me get the rosewater," I whisper.

Inside the tent he sits up to make room. Hold the bowl and the cloth, crawl in and it's like sitting low in high fields hidden away, except there isn't even sky, no opening at all.

"It's like a coffin, that's what," he'd said when he could talk.

"A coffin is long and thin," I told him, "with a lid."

"Mine has a ceiling," Warwick said.

Inside everything is clean and white and dry; every day we change the white bottom sheet and he isn't allowed any covers. He's sitting up—I still can't see him in the dark; even the netting looks black, so I find him, hand forehead nose throat.

"Can't you see me? There's a moon, I see you fine."

"Then you've turned into a bat. I'll see in a moment, it was light in the kitchen."

"Mam?"

"Mam and three lamps. She's rolling bandages this hour of the night. She doesn't sleep when you don't."

"I can't sleep."

"I know."

He only sleeps in daytime when he can hear people making noise. At night he wakes up in silence, in the narrow black room, in bandages in the tent. For a while when the doctor bled him he was too weak to yell for someone.

"I won't need bandages much longer," he says.

"A little longer," I tell him.

"I should be up walking. I wonder if I can walk; like before I wondered if I could see."

"Of course you can walk, you've only been in bed two weeks, and a few days before upstairs—"

"I don't remember when they moved me here, so don't it seem like always I been here?"

Pa and Dennis and Claude and Mam moved him, all wearing gloves and their forearms wrapped in gauze I took off them later and burned in the woodstove.

"Isn't always. You had deep sleeps in the fever, you remember wrong."

I start at his feet which are nearly healed, with the sponge and the cool water. Water we took from the rain barrel and scented with torn roses, the petals pounded with a pestle and strained, since the doctor said not to use soap.

The worst week I bathed him at night so he wouldn't get terrified alone. He was delirious and didn't know when he slept or woke. When I touched him with the cloth he made such whispers, such inside sounds; they weren't even words but had a cadence like sentences. When he whispered them to me it was all right; I wasn't scared, but that one noon his fever was highest and the room itself like an oven—he shouted, on and on—Mam made everyone pray, even the men called in from work in the fields. Satan was inside Warwick. That is not God's language, she said, Satan is trying to take him. She yelled louder than Warwick as though he might hear if she shouted the devil down: *He delighteth not in the strength, He taketh not pleasure in the legs of a man, the Lord taketh pleasure in them that fear Him. . . . Fear him! hope in His Mercy, He casteth forth His ice like morsels—*

I was rubbing Warwick with alcohol to take the sweat, he was wet and smelled of poison, his legs arms eyes all bandaged and hands and legs tied down so he wouldn't thrash and make his raw skin bleed—I was terrified there in the hot narrow room, sun in the windows horribly bright. Voices in the kitchen, the other side of the wall. *Thou hast made him lower than angels . . . he did fly up,* Mam shouted, and Warwick in the darkness in his secret place, all round about him like black water boiling in the dark. I could see him vanishing like something sucked down a hole, like fire ducked into a slit. If he could hear them praying, if he could feel this heat and the heat of his fever, blind as he was then in bandages, and tied, if he could still think, he'd think he was in hell. I poured the alcohol over him, and the water from the basin, I was bent close his face just when he stopped raving and I thought he had died. He said a word.

"Bessie," he said.

Bless me, I heard. I knelt with my mouth at his ear, in the sweat, in the horrible smell of the poison. "Warwick," I said. He was there, tentative and weak, a boy waking up after sleeping in the blackness three days. "Stay here, Warwick. Warwick."

I heard him say the word again, and it was my name, clearly.

"Bessie," he said.

So I answered him. "Yes, I'm here. Stay here."

Later he told me he slept a hundred years, swallowed in a vast black belly like Jonah, no time anymore, no sense but strange dreams without pictures. He thought he was dead, he said, and the moment he came back he spoke the only word he'd remembered in the dark.

Sixteen years later, when he did die, in the mine— did he say a word again, did he say that word? Trying to come back. The second time, I think he went like a streak. I had the color silver in my mind. A man from Coalton told us about the cave-in. The man rode out on a horse, a bay mare, and he galloped the mare straight across the fields to the porch instead of taking

the road. I was sitting on the porch and saw him coming from a ways off. I stood up as he came closer. I
knew the news was Warwick, and that whatever had
happened was over. I had no words in my mind, just
the color silver, everywhere. The fields looked silver
too just then, the way the sun slanted. The grass was
tall and the mare moved through it up to her chest,
like a powerful swimmer. I did not call anyone else
until the man arrived and told me, breathless, that
Warwick and two others were trapped, probably suffo-
cated, given up for dead. The man, a Mr. Forbes, was
surprised at my composure. I simply nodded; the news
came to me like an echo. I had not thought of that
moment in years—the moment Warwick's fever broke
and I heard him speak—but it returned in an instant.
Having once felt that disappearance, even so long before, I was prepared. Memory does not work according to time. I was twelve years old, perceptive, impres-
sionable, in love with Warwick as a brother and sister
can be in love. I loved him then as one might love
one's twin, without a thought. After that summer I
understood too much. I don't mean I was ashamed; I
was not. But no love is innocent once it has recognized
its own existence.

At eighteen, I went away to a finishing school in
Lynchburg. The summer I came back, foolishly, I ran
away west. I eloped partially because Warwick found
fault with anyone who courted me, and made a case
against him to Mam. The name of the man I left with
is unimportant. I do not really remember his face. He
was blond but otherwise he did resemble Warwick—
in his movements, his walk, his way of speaking. All
told, I was in his company eight weeks. We were traveling, staying in hotels. He'd told me he was in textiles
but it seemed actually he gambled at cards and roulette. He had a sickness for the roulette wheel, and

other sicknesses. I could not bear to stand beside him in the gambling parlors; I hated the noise and the smoke, the perfumes mingling, the clackings of the wheels like speeded-up clocks and everyone's eyes following numbers. Often I sat in a hotel room with a blur of noise coming through the floor, and imagined the vast space of the barn around me: dark air filling a gold oval, the tall beams, the bird sounds ghostly, like echoes. The hay, ragged heaps that spilled from the mow in pieces and fell apart.

The man who was briefly my husband left me in St. Louis. Warwick came for me; he made a long journey in order to take me home. A baby boy was born the following September. It was decided to keep my elopement and divorce, and the pregnancy itself, secret. Our doctor, a country man and friend of the family, helped us forge a birth certificate stating that Warwick was the baby's father. We invented a name for his mother, a name unknown in those parts, and told that she'd abandoned the baby to us. People lived so far from one another, in isolation, that such deceit was possible. My boy grew up believing I was his aunt and Warwick his father, but Warwick could not abide him. To him, the child was living reminder of my abasement, my betrayal in ever leaving the farm.

Lately I have a dream. As is true in fact, I am the last one left. The farmhouse is deserted but still standing; I walk away from it. There is mist from the creek and the moist smell of day lilies, mustard bitters of their furred sepals broken in the black ivy. Thick beds of the dark-veined leaves are a tangle in the undergrowth. There, in the thicket where I fought with Warwick, I find the yellow rope, bleached pale as rain in those leaves. The frayed fibers are a white fuzz along the ground. I kneel down to touch the leaves, and the dirt beneath is cool as cellar air, pliable as sand. I dig a

hole, as though a grave is there, a grave I will discover.
Cards I find, and a knife. And the voice of a preacher,
wet and charred: *One man among a thousand I found, but
a woman among all these I have not found.*

The funeral was held at the house. Men from the
mine saw to it Warwick was laid out in Coalton, then
they brought the box to the farm on a lumber wagon.
The lid was kept shut. That was the practice then; if
a man died in the mines his coffin was closed for ser-
vices, nailed shut, even if the man was unmarked.

The day after Warwick's funeral, all the family was
leaving back to their homesteads, having seen each
other in a confused picnic of food and talk and sorrow-
ful conjecture. Half the sorrow was Warwick alive and
half was Warwick dead. His dying would make an end
of the farm. I would leave now for Bellington, where,
in a year, I would meet another man. Mam and Pa
would go to live with Claude and his wife. But it was
more than losing the farm that puzzled and saddened
everyone; no one knew who Warwick was, really. They
said it was hard to believe he was inside the coffin, with
the lid nailed shut that way. Touch the box, anywhere,
with the flat of your hand, I told them. They did, and
stopped that talk.

The box was thick pine boards, pale white wood; I
felt I could fairly look through it like water into his
face, like he was lying in a piece of water on top of the
parlor table. Touching the nailed lid you felt first the
cool slide of new wood on your palm, and a second
later, the depth—a heaviness, the box was so deep it
went clear to the center of the earth, his body con-
tained there like a big caged wind. Something inside,
palpable as the different air before flash rains, with
clouds blown and air clicking before the crack of
downpour.

I treated the box as though it were living: it had to

accustom itself to the strange air of the house, of the parlor, a room kept for weddings and death. The box was simply there on the table, long and pure like some deeply asleep, dangerous animal. The stiff damask draperies at the parlor windows looked as though they were about to move, gold tassels at the hems suspended and still.

The morning before the service most of the family had been in Coalton, seeing to what is done at a death. I had been alone in the house with the coffin churning what air there was to breathe. I had dressed in best clothes as though for a serious, bleak suitor. The room was just lighted with sunrise, window shades pulled halfway, their cracked sepia lit from behind. One locust began to shrill as I took a first step across the floor; somehow one had gotten into the room. The piercing, fast vibration was very loud in the still morning: suddenly I felt myself smaller, cramped as I bent over Warwick inside his white tent of netting, his whole body afloat below me on the narrow bed, his white shape in the loose bandages seeming to glow in dusk light while beyond the row of open windows hundreds of locusts sang a ferocious pattering. I could scarcely see the parlor anymore. My vision went black for a moment, not black but dark green, like the color of the dusk those July weeks years before.